MAI TAIS AND GOODBYES

J. A. WYNTERS

*To those who leap and follow their dreams,
you will never regret being brave.*

<u>Glossary:</u>

Eema - Mum
Aba - Dad
Savta - Grandmother
Motek – Sweetheart/ Darling
Sheli – Mine
Bottle'o – Bottle Shop
Ute – Pickup Truck
Esky – Ice box/ Cooler
Snags - Sausages
Tradie – Works as a tradesman
Sparkie – Electrician
Limp Bacon – Abi's favourite fictional vintage band from the 80's that only released one album.

Chapter One

Seth

Love is only for the fools and the weak.

But as of today, I'll be neither. I stuff my T-shirts into my duffle bag as the sting of betrayal surges through me. I'm possessed by anger and anguish so deep, I'm drowning in my own fucking misery.

How could I have been so blind? How did I let everything slip out of my fingers? Was I not good enough? Loyal enough? Giving enough? What does *he* have that I don't? What was she looking for in his bed that she couldn't find in mine? Why?

She told me it wasn't the sex, she told me that that came later. And I don't know what's worse, knowing that she found comfort in another man's bed or in his company? That his companionship was better than mine? That he made her smile and laugh more. That his absence made her ache, whereas my presence gave her nothing. It made no difference, I still wanted to murder him, break him, attack all the pieces till there was nothing left of him.

She didn't spare me the details. Each of her words, a knife

in my throat, till all I was breathing was pain. Until it hurt so bad that I screamed and yelled and she ran away.

To him.

Into another man's arms.

Shock. As if I have fallen off a steep cliff and landed on my back, the impact rendering my body useless. My lungs gush out every wisp of air inside them, leaving me struggling to inhale and exhale. I'm stunned, my brain faltering, my thoughts trying to catch up with the impact.

I stand in place staring at the door Jess slammed as she left, till my adrenaline kicks in and suddenly my very survival feels threatened and all I can do is fight or run.

I look around our apartment, the walls mocking me. Rage surges through my veins. I did everything right—*everything*—and still I wasn't good enough for her. Her emotional indifference has weaponized my body, setting it on fire; a hot burning rage that wants to harm. It pumps through me, pulsing with my quickened heartbeat. Acid burns my stomach and seeks to erupt from my mouth in the form of profanity and abuse. Instead I grunt as I smash my fist through the wall, craving the physical pain that would alleviate some of the burn inside of me.

Plaster explodes around my fist as it digs in. The next punch is accompanied by a savage growl that rips from me, tearing my insides as it rattles the knives her betrayal planted in my chest.

I decorate the wall with my pain, a collection of ugly broken holes.

Breathless, I look at the damage; my heart smashing in my chest, the adrenalin soaking every part of me.

There was no one to fight.

I guess it was time to consider option number two.

I toss my bag over my shoulder and give the apartment a quick once over, making sure I didn't leave anything that was mine.

That mattered.

She can keep the furniture, the pictures, even the fucking cat—they don't mean shit any more. I just want what's mine.

I'll never get my two years back, but I'm not leaving my Star Wars LEGO minifig collection. She always said they were infantile. Maybe that should have been the first sign that we were never meant to be.

I'll call Lachie later and get him to grab what he can before she gets back and sees the damage I caused. The wall doesn't even begin to mirror my smashed insides.

I throw my bag on the passenger seat and start the car. Some love song croons from the radio and I punch it off. My hands grip the steering wheel till my bruised, aching knuckles bleed white and sting. My skin feels too tight for my body and everything hurts. I'm lost and I have no idea where to go.

My head falls back onto the headrest and I stare at the stupid blue skies, perfect and clear till a plane slices through it, leaving behind a long white scar. It fades as I stare at it and put the car into gear.

I know exactly where I'm going.

Chapter Two

Seth

I leave my ute at the long-term parking without any real idea of what I'm doing, grab my bag and walk off to the departure terminal.

I'm not in a hurry to be anywhere. My schedule has suddenly freed right up—not that Lachie and Jake will agree—but they'll have to deal with it. For now. My fingers brush over the ring in my pocket, I ignore the weight of it and bury all that deep inside for later. The refund will pay for the stupid mistakes I'm about to make.

Fuck it. You only live once right?

The terminal is busy, loud and crowded with people getting on with their own colourful lives. It's like walking into a swarm. A constant hum of excited conversation and pounding feet on the cold tiled floor as people rush around me. The air is laden with a combination of anticipation and boredom. It feels like everyone knows their place, everyone has a direction.

I scan the terminal and spot a young couple holding hands, looking dreamily at one another. My stomach churns and my fists clench, looking for something to hit.

I shake it off, internalizing and promising myself I'll deal with it all later—once the rage has subsided and I can make sense of it all. Right now, I need to keep moving.

I make my way to the plasma screens displaying departure times and scan the flight schedules, not entirely sure what I'm looking for.

Distance.

I let out a long exhale. That's what I need right now. Everything in this fucking city makes me think of Jess. And my failure.

I grind my teeth and look at the board going through my options. There's a flight to Phuket in six hours.

Eight-hour flight, sunny destination, and somewhere I've never been.

Perfect.

I swipe my phone and buy a ticket online while still standing by the screen. Once I get the email confirmation, I look around. People are lined up at the check-in desks with suitcases and baggage, some are sipping coffee at overpriced cafés, others are saying their goodbyes, their affectionate smiles and touches make me cringe. I turn away and make my way to the security line—seems like I have a lot of time to kill.

I clear security and passport control and step into the duty-free. The place looks more like a shopping mall than an airport. Floor to ceiling windows let in too much light and reflect off the white tiles, the scent of coffee and spicy food mingles with detergent and creates a unique perfume that's almost comforting.

I spend the next hour making myself a tourist at the airside shops, rifling through best sellers and magazines, examining exotic liqueurs and unfamiliar chocolates. Jess would have loved them. The thought pinches and I shove it down as I move away from the shelves, out of the shop, and back into the flooded corridor.

Two currents flow in opposite directions. People coming and going. I feel like an island in a river of humanity. Isolated and totally alone. The creeping sense of grief and denial follow me like a shadow.

I scan the corridor till I see a green flashing light. It hangs over an Irish pub which sticks out like a sore thumb surrounded by souvenir shops full of stuffed koalas and boomerangs. I check my watch and shrug at the early hour; it's after 12 p.m. somewhere in the world, and I can use a beer or a few shots of whiskey.

The paint on the thick, red door is flecked and has chipped in places, I push through, and step inside. The bright light of the terminal instantly dimmed by low hung lights, the hum of humanity replaced by background rock music, laughter and murmured conversations.

The place is packed. Businessmen having their preflight drinks and overindulgent meals, young guys drinking their breakfasts, and couples sharing a bite to eat. I scan the room and find two deserted stools at the end of the bar. I weave my way over and sit, resting my backpack on the seat next to mine.

The barwoman's long face seems haggard and tired as she serves an elderly man a pint. He thanks her and she gives him a well-trained smile that's as empty as the glass he left behind. She places it on the washing rack then spots me. She waddles over, her wide rounded shape inches away from the counter and the fridges closing in on her on either side.

She drops a menu in front of me and recites the day's specials in a bored monotone. No greeting, no emotion, an overworked robot in a dead-end job.

"I'll give you a couple of minutes." She walks off without actually giving me a chance to ask for anything.

I clench my jaw, irritation skittering along my skin, and scan the grease stained menu. It's pretty standard. The usual array of steaks, fish and chips, and assortment of burgers. I'm deep into the burger selection when an accented feminine voice lures me away from my reading.

"Excuse me, is this seat taken?" My head snaps over my shoulder to see a woman standing just behind me. Hair tied up in a tight bun and shimmering chocolate brown eyes, which boomerang from my face to the stool occupied by my bag.

"I guess not." I grab my bag off the stool and let it drop down to the floor by my feet, and she slips into the seat beside me.

"Thank you." She smiles at me, but it doesn't touch the rest of her face. Her hidden pain evident in the crease of her brow and the downward curve of her eyes.

"Want to see the menu?" I push it in her direction and her full lips curve up a little more.

"Thanks." She takes it from me and her eyes glance over the words.

It gives me a chance to study her. Chestnut colored hair frames her delicate face, her high cheekbones lightly rouged, and her lips coated in lipstick that glistens in the dim lights. She's wearing a fading Iron Maiden T-shirt that has seen too many washes and hangs loosely around her.

The barwoman notices her and makes her way back over. "You two ready to order?" She barks in her dry sourly voice.

"Oh, we're not to get—" I start.

"Let me give you another minute." She rolls her eyes and makes to walk away.

"Wait," my new neighbor calls out, the barwoman turns back and looks at her expectantly, "I'd like two shots of tequila and a glass of house red, and my friend here will have a pint of your house lager."

"We can't serve alcohol before 12 p.m. unless accompanied by a meal." The barwoman's voice wearisome, as if she's repeated it too many times this morning already.

"Okay, then we will have two house burgers with that."

She turns to me and cocks her head, an eyebrow raising in question.

"Yeah, house burger sounds fine," I nod.

The barwoman grabs the menu from the bar and rings up the order. She brings the card machine over, and before I have a chance to reach for my wallet my new lady-friend has paid for our food and drinks. The barwoman slinks away to the back, and I turn to face the newcomer who'd just bought me the breakfast I probably needed.

"Thank you." It comes out as confused as I feel.

"Ugh," she screws her eyes shut for a second and when she opens them again, the pain behind them floor me, "I must come across as a complete nutter."

"Well, maybe a little."

Her mouth twists into a little smile, and she drags her hands down her face. "The drink was meant as a thank you for letting me sit down, and well, she wouldn't bring it without the burger…"

"I'm not old-fashioned or anything, but I usually like to know the name of a woman that's buying *me* drinks at 11 a.m."

She chuckles and extends a lithe hand, I accept and we shake, "Abigail, but my friends call me Abi."

"Seth."

"Nice to meet you, Seth."

Her accent is confusing, and I try to gauge where she might be from. The barwoman places our shots down, followed by my pint and Abi's wine. She reaches for her shot and waits for me to do the same.

Fuck it, it's been a shit day.

We both lick the small cavity between thumb and finger and Abi dusts it with salt.

"Cheers." She lifts her shot glass to mine, and a few drops splutter on the counter when they meet in a soft clink

I lick the salt; it stings my tongue and dries my throat. I

throw my head back and let the tequila slide down. It burns and I feel the warmth as it smashes into my stomach and sloshes around, heating my empty insides. I shove the wedge of lemon into my mouth and screw my eyes shut as the juice sinks into my lips and zings my tongue, erasing the harsh alcohol flavour.

I smash my empty shot glass onto the bar and watch Abi. Her face is all scrunched up as she sucks on her lemon wedge.

She pulls it out of her mouth which is twisted, then grabs her wine glass and takes a big gulp.

"Blegh," she says, her face scrunching and her shoulders shivering. "*That* was a bad idea."

"Tequila?"

"Tequila with a red wine chaser," she smiles. "I should have gone with the white."

"Or another tequila?" I joke.

"That's not a bad idea." Her eyes light up and she waves down to the barwoman then holds up her empty shot glass and two fingers.

I guess we're having another shot.

I sip my beer trying to erase the sour lemon flavor and ease the burning in my belly. The lemon mixes with the beer and changes its bitter flavor into something citrusy and fresh.

"So now that you bought me breakfast, are you planning on getting me drunk and taking advantage of me?"

She squints in my direction as if considering my question. "Well, I guess it's the least I could do."

I scoff as her lips twitch with a shy smile. But before I can ask anything else, the barwoman lumbers over with our shots and places them in front of us. Abigail grabs the salt and licks the junction between her thumb and finger, and I pretend not to notice how my dick flicks. I ignore the feeling, do the same, then give her my hand. She peppers the salt over the wet area and holds her shot glass up. We clink a second time and I tilt my head backwards, letting the tequila slide down my throat. It doesn't burn as much the second time around. I suck on my lemon, discard it, and turn back to face her.

"What brings you here, Abigail?"

"I prefer Abi."

"Ok, Abi."

She looks around as if making sure the coast is clear then leans in so that she could whisper in a conspiratorial tone, "I'm an inter galactic smuggler running away from a tyrannical space commander."

She says it so seriously it takes me a whole second to register her words. "I find that hard to believe." I keep a straight face.

"Why is that?"

"Cause, you've basically admitted to being a pirate, but you ordered tequila and not rum." I throw at her.

"I'm a smuggler. Anyway, it's a common misconception that rum is all that pirates drink. Not to mention if I was one, I wouldn't want to give myself away." She winks at me.

"I guess that would have been quite telling."

"Aye," She tips her head and I can't help but chuckle at her ridiculousness. "What about you, Seth? What brings you to this luxury bar on this fine day?"

Thoughts of Jess flicker around my mind, I push them back and decide to play along, "I'm a bounty hunter sent out to capture an elusive and dangerous mark."

"Oh?" Her eyebrows lift a little and she turns more towards me, her knee brushes my thigh as she does.

"A treacherous mark that's been wanted by the Space Federation for years. Many others have tried and failed before me."

"I see," she says, "and have you found your mark?"

"It's hard to tell, I was told she drinks rum." She bursts out laughing and it's a lovely heartfelt sound, like it comes from deep inside her and is totally real. I feel a flutter in my stomach at making her laugh.

With that, I gesture to the barwoman who rolls over, seemingly tired of us interrupting her workday.

"Can I have a shot of rum, please?"

"Which one?" she says on a sigh and I shrug.

"Best one you have."

"Sure." She sneers and waddles off to grab a shot glass. She takes a bottle from a top shelf and fills the glass before setting it in front of us.

Abi eyes the shot suspiciously and leans closer again, "Do you think Bertha over there spit polishes these shot glasses?" She juts her chin towards the barwoman standing on the opposite side of the bar, throwing us sideways glances.

I choke on a mouthful of beer as I laugh, "Bertha?"

"Sure, before she worked here, she was well on her way as an up and coming lawyer, working hard to become a partner in her firm. She gave everything up for her career and when —finally—the day came and she was made partner, she found out that the place was going bankrupt and she was brought in as the fall girl for all their illegal activities. They destroyed her career and her life. Distraught, she piled on the weight, stopped shaving her chin, and sought out a new career here where she can judge people all day based on their appearances and carry out her own brand of kitchen law by either spitting or not spitting on their food and polishing the glasses…"

I slam my beer down onto the bar and glare at her, "That's my future wife you've just insulted." She stills and her eyes grow wide, "and it wasn't a law firm, it was a car wash. They said she used it as a front for laundering her money."

There's another short pause between us before we burst out laughing.

"I'm just kidding," I say when our laughter dies down, "we're already married."

She laughs again and elbows me, the gesture feels way too familiar and comfortable, and I wonder why I enjoy it so much instead of jerking away like I should be.

"Sorry for insulting your lovely wife," her mouth twitches at the edge, "I've always wanted to be a writer."

"Well, based on the narrative you just came up with, I think it's a good time to give up. You clearly don't have any flair for storytelling," I shrug. "You should stick to being a pirate. In fact, you haven't touched your rum."

She huffs, "I won't fall for your cheap tricks bounty hunter. I told you, I don't drink rum." Her hand edges toward the shot glass before she turns up her nose, grabs her glass of wine and takes a large sip.

'Bertha' steps towards us with our plates of food, it smells like two-week-old fryer oil and diluted sweat. I wonder if she's spat in it.

As she places the plates on the bar, she points a sausage like finger towards the back of the room, "That booth just opened up if you want to grab it."

I turn to see an empty booth on the other end of the room. When I turn to look at Abi, she shrugs, smiles, and says, "Yes!"

Before I can say anything else, she grabs her plate and her bag and darts towards the unoccupied space.

Chapter Three

Abi

I don't look back as I head for the booth but find myself hoping Seth is following me. That is, if he doesn't think I am a complete nut job yet. I cringe inwardly, thinking of the way I must have come across in the last half hour—forcing tequila down his throat and pretending to be a pirate. To his credit, he played along. He's been a distraction. A very handsome one if I'm being honest.

Wild dirty blonde hair pushed haphazardly to one side over his hazel and honey eyes, a sexy smile that softens his prominent jaw, hidden under a mass of short dark stubble.

I slide into the booth, set my bag down and look up to see Seth set the shot of rum in the middle of the table. Making sure I watch, he drags it deliberately slowly towards my plate.

"You forgot your shot," he says, then casually drops his bag off his shoulder, slips into the booth, and places his food down.

I make a show of studying it and grab a chip instead, "I told you, I don't drink rum."

"Pity," he smiles as he grabs his burger and takes a large

bite. Sauce coats his top lip and he licks it off before setting the burger down. My stomach does a long slow roll and I look away wondering what the hell is wrong with me.

"So, how does one become a galactic pirate on the run?" he asks between bites, not missing a beat.

"You know, you piss off a few tyrants and start a smuggling ring. It's surprisingly easy…"

"Drink rum?"

"Never." We both deadpan though I can tell he's battling a smile. "What about you? How did you end up becoming a bounty hunter?"

"Well, after a failed career as a prima ballerina and assistant gynecologist, the only option left was bounty hunting."

"Seems like the logical progression."

He shrugs, "That's how I saw it."

I bite down a smile and hide behind my burger, taking another bite. I'm thankful for the coating of tomato sauce and mustard mayo, which heavily disguises the taste of the dry meat.

A comfortable silence falls between us as we eat our food. It gives me more time to look at this man that I've somehow dragged into sharing a greasy breakfast with me and hasn't run away from my crazy. Talking to him has quieted the turmoil that's been raging inside me since this morning. I can't believe how much can change in twenty-four hours. I put my burger down needing to drown away the wave of feelings about to smash into me and grab my wine. My hand shakes as I put it to my mouth and the red liquid sloshes down my chin and onto my shirt.

Seth looks up from his food, "Hands not very steady for a pirate, are they? Rum withdrawals?"

I'm grateful for his humor and even more so that he's remained sitting down.

"I never withdraw from anything," I wink at him and his

mouth falls a little open as I stand up. "I'm just going to go wash it off."

His look lingers on my shirt and his brow furrows, "Yeah, would hate to stain that artifact."

"I'll have you know it is, in fact, a rare collectible."

"Keep telling yourself that." He chuckles and returns to his food as I push out of the booth and make my way to the bathroom.

I smash through the door, lock it, then grip onto the white basin needing something steady to hold me up. The emotions came out of nowhere. I was fine. Seth was keeping me occupied and all of a sudden the silence pushed the pain back to the surface; like a volcano has erupted inside me and everything is burned and scalded and agonising.

I stare at myself in the mirror and shake my head. A stray line of tomato sauce stuck to my cheek and my hair frazzled, the flyways standing in all directions like tiny antennas on my head. My shirt has a black splotch right between my breasts, coating Eddie's face. I look haggard. No wonder he bought the pirate bit so easily. A ghost of a smile touches my lips as I turn on the faucet and wait for the water to warm a little before I wash my face again and again and again. I let the water stream down my face, little rivulets run beneath my eyes and make their way to the tip of my nose and down my chin. They dampen the fire inside me, but only just.

I find some paper towel and dry off before dabbing it under the water and washing my shirt, the wet stain spreads across my chest and I spend the next five minutes standing under the hand drier wondering if Seth will still be there when I get out.

I check myself out in the mirror again and let loose my hair. I pull it back in a neater ponytail trying to capture all my flyways and slap on another thin coat of lipstick that's all but disappeared between the drinks and the food.

I check myself one more time, not entirely happy with

what I see when I hear her voice echo inside me. *'You're gorgeous sweetheart, even with your messy hair and tired eyes. It's your insides that make you shine.'* My lips stretch into a thin line and my heart constricts. I hear her so clearly, as if she was standing right next to me. The tears brim again. I shake my head, take a deep breath and get out of the bathroom before Seth thinks I've run out on him or worse, thinks a rival bounty hunter got to me first. The thought helps to shake me from my mood.

When I make my way back to the table, he's scrolling through his phone but puts it down and smiles as soon as I sit down.

"I googled you," he says it so nonchalantly, I do a double take as I look at him till I realize he's joking. "Not much information on a pirate called Abigail."

"Makes a nice change of pace," I throw back at him. "Great to meet someone who isn't after my shipments, my vast wealth, or a reward for my capture."

"I didn't say that." He winks. Before I can answer he gestures toward the shot glass still resting between us, "You were gone a while, you must be thirsty again."

"You're right, I am thirsty. House red please, to replace the one I decorated my shirt with.

You're buying."

His right eyebrow shoots up and I give him my best smile. "Pretty sure I bought you a shot of rum."

"Pretty sure I told you I don't drink rum."

He smirks and stands, "Rum then?"

I check my watch, three hours till my flight.

He notices, "What time is your flight?"

"I still have a few hours."

He smiles and his face lights up, making my stomach come alive with a flutter of butterflies, when really I shouldn't be doing any of this. I bat the thought away. Fuck it, any distraction is a good distraction and I need one desperately. Of course, it helps if it comes wrapped up in a package that looks like Seth. I watch his swagger as he walks towards the bar and get to appreciate how his jeans mold perfectly to his tight ass. I try to ignore the kind of distraction I'd like Seth to be and concentrate on the last few bites of my burger. Still, I can't help but to keep staring at his perfect ass.

Chapter Four

Seth

A few shots, beers and cups of coffee later, and I find myself totally mesmerized and drawn to this unique, mysterious creature known as Abi. She's very guarded and her pirate persona has completely taken over, but I don't mind. Spending this time with her, I realize that I haven't laughed as much or had as much fun with another person in months, maybe longer.

I know there are still a million and one things I don't know about her; but I'm quickly learning that she's fun and witty, and I'm enjoying making her laugh and making her eyes light up, being the one who makes her hands shoot up to her mouth to cover up her few snorts that ended up with both of us falling into fits of laughter. She's free and easy and seems careless in the best way, which is why the last few hours have flown by.

Every time thoughts of Jess slide to the front of my mind, I can't help but compare the two of them. I wonder more and more where we went wrong and why it never felt like this with her. I don't want to think of our time as wasted, we still had good times. Maybe being with her was a long lesson in teaching me what didn't work for either of us. I sigh and look at Abi's lit up face, it's hard to ignore how gorgeous she is.

She checks her watch and her lips curve downwards, "I have to go."

I feel a sudden pang of heaviness around my body and realize I don't want her to go. I don't want my time with this mystery woman to end. I check my watch and frown, "Me too."

"Where are you heading to, pirate?"

"A land far away, where smugglers are welcome with open arms."

"How will I find you again?"

"If you're half the bounty hunter you say you are, you'll find me." With that she stands up, grabs the shot of Rum, downs it and winks as she slams it back on the table.

"I knew it!" I bolt up from my seat, but she's already muscling her way through the bar and heading for the door.

"Abi," I call after her, all the heads in the bar turn towards me, but I don't give a shit. I grab my bag and it snags on something. I bend to unlatch it, and when I look up again, she's gone.

I run out of the bar, the sudden bright light sears my eyes and I blink it away then look up and down the crowded duty free. No sign of her, like she's been swallowed by the swarm of humanity packed into the building. Regret and disappointment swirl around me, colliding in a strange fight for domination. I grind my teeth and swear at myself for not getting her number, then reluctantly make my way down to my departure gate.

My stomach churns as I walk down the corridor. I check my passport over as anger bubbles under my skin at my inability to take a risk. Who the hell lets a girl like that go without at least getting her full name? I keep walking on the sleek white tiles, moving forward, looking ahead, leaving behind all my memories.

I stand at the gate, leaning against the wall. Wave after wave of irritation washes over me as I question my IQ. Other passengers mill around waiting for us to board. My sudden itch to leave Melbourne has disappeared, replaced by a tug to find a chestnut-colour haired pirate who, for some strange reason, has piqued my interest and snagged all my attention.

There's movement around the counter where three air hostesses start talking in urgent hushed tones. One keeps listening to a walkie talkie and as they stand around, their mouths stretch into thin lines and eyes roll and I know that something is going on.

After a few more minutes their tight group breaks up and the one with the walkie talkie disappears behind a security door, while the taller of the two remaining hostesses grabs the microphone. The annoying chime of an announcement rings through the terminal and the hostess starts to speak.

"Ladies and gentlemen, the captain has just informed me that our flight has been delayed by an hour. Please keep an eye out on the board for our next departure and boarding time."

As expected, the line of people already standing and waiting to board erupt in an annoyed hum like an angry hive; but they don't attack, they disperse—slowly and begrudgingly. Some return to empty seats while others slug away back to duty free. I'm about to do the same when I see a woman, her chestnut-coloured hair in a tight bun and her nose stuck in a book. She doesn't move as the crowd thins out and I inch closer, taking her in.

Her legs are pulled up and the book rests on her knees as she reads. I take a few careful steps forwards and my heart skips a few ridiculous beats as I realise it's *her*.

I make my way carefully behind her and lean over so that my lips are a few inches from her ear, "I have you now!"

She startles and twists—almost head butting me as she does—her arms up and ready to smack something. Her expression changes from alarmed to confused to relaxed to hesitant. It all happens so fast, it's like watching a firework display on her face.

"You followed me." It's not quite a question or a statement, but I still detect an undercurrent of uncertainty in her voice.

"Well, I am the best bounty hunter in the universe." I wink at her but can see the game is over when her expression doesn't change. "Also, this is my flight." Just to appease her, I pull out my phone and show her my booking.

Her brow furrows for a second as she takes in this new information, "So, you're not stalking me?"

"No more than I did my last victim," I deadpan.

She blinks a few times as if processing what I said, "Was she also a pirate?"

"Yeah nah, she was a good girl who went to deliver cookies to her grandmother and was never seen again." She laughs at last and relaxes a little. "May I sit down?"

She thinks about it for a beat, then nods waving to the empty seats beside her. I put my bag down and extend my hand out to her. "Seth Taylor."

She puts her hand in mine, much like she did earlier today, "Abigail Tal."

"Nice to meet you. Again."

Her lips tilt in a crooked smile and my cock twitches in my pants. I pull my hand away, instantly missing the softness of her hand.

"So, when you're not bounty hunting, what do you do?"

"I'm in construction," I say and rub my rough hands together.

"Sounds fascinating," she says.

"It's not. It's manual labour in all sorts of weather, it takes its toll on your body and ruins all your clothes."

"Have you considered working naked?"

"It's crossed my mind a few times, but when my clients started throwing $1 coins at me, I had to quit. I bruise easily."

She giggles and snatches a look down at my groin which I totally notice. "Did you just check me out?" I call her out and red leaks into her cheeks. "My eyes are up here, sweetheart," I tut at her, driving it in.

"What?" She crosses her arms over her chest, "Of course not! Have you seen yourself?"

"Well, I haven't had more than four complaints about it today," I smirk, and the red intensifies in her cheeks. We burst into laughter.

"What about you?"

"Me? No, I've never considered working naked."

"That's unfortunate," I mumble as I make sure she notices me checking her out. She shoves me on the shoulder and the gesture is sweet in its uninhibited casualness. Like she's done it a hundred times before, like it's the most natural thing in the world between us.

She clears her throat and tries to recompose herself, "I'm actually an air hostess."

"Oh, so why are you not in the jump seat?"

She looks down and I feel like I've hit a nerve, "It's a personal flight, and this isn't the airline I work at."

"Personal? To Thailand? Are you meeting anyone?"

"Yes."

My stomach dips, "Is he a friend? Is he as handsome as me?"

"Well, my sister has been called a lot of things before, handsome is not one." She bites down a little smile, and I realize she's teasing me. I like it.

My mood lightens up instantly, "So a family vacation? A wedding?" I know I shouldn't pry, but now that I've almost lost her once, I have the urge to get as much out of her as I can.

Her lips drop and her eyes turn a shade darker. "Funeral actually," she clears her throat, and I feel like a complete asshole.

"Your latest victim?" I try desperately to dig myself out of the hole I just dug.

Her mouth twitches and her eyes find mine, "Something like that." She exhales the pain she's hiding, "What about you? What takes you to Thailand?"

The question is like an icicle down to my core. It freezes the humiliation, the pain, the anger. I feel like an ice sculpture, but not extravagant and beautiful, rather hacked to pieces and mutilated.

"I need to get away."

"Why? Bounty hunting taking its toll?"

I suck in a sharp breath and grip the back of my neck, "Yeah, my latest victim managed to get away..." that's *mostly* telling her the truth.

"Tough break." She elbows me playfully and our eyes lock, and for a moment, the whole world stands still and the terminal fills with charged electricity that hums between us.

I unlatch my eyes from hers, breaking the moment, "Want to get out of here?"

"Sure," she nods and we both stand, grab our hand luggage and head back towards the duty-free area. We fall into the stream of other people milling about. As I keep step with Abi, I realize I don't feel as lonely as I did just six hours ago.

Chapter Five

Abi

Seth is a strange balm to the constant ache I've felt since I lost her. I've always felt that it's an odd thing to say, when someone died, they're not lost … you know exactly where they are.' Well, providing you buried them that is. But she was never conventional, and she never wanted roots—not the ones that kept her in one place forever. She wanted a home, somewhere she could always come back to and she made us that home; a beautiful happy place, where we felt safe and cherished. But she never wanted to stay put, and she rarely did. She lived her life till her very last breath, and I wish so often I was braver just like her. Freer to allow myself to make stupid mistakes and random choices. Today, of all days, feels like a strange day to start.

I spot a book shop and make my way inside. I love book shops and, even though this one feels generic with it's too bright lights and too clean floors, it still holds the same sentiments. Polished shelves displaying inky treasures, holding inside their covers the expression of human souls that echo our own.

I wind my way around the magazine shelves, my fingers

feathering a few hard covers as I make my way to the display on the back wall. Hundreds of books look back at me. At the back, the noise of the terminal is a dull hum, and I take a long breath. Despite the commercial and less personalized feel of this shop, it still smells like freshly printed papers and polished shelves with an undertone of endless emotions that leak from the pages.

"See anything you like?" Seth's voice cuts through my thoughts.

"I don't know yet." He smiles at me and I turn my attention back to the bookshelf. A few covers grab my interest and I pull book after book off the shelf, flipping them over and reading the blurb waiting for something to capture me. When I look up, I find Seth studying me as intently as I studied the last book I replaced on the shelf.

"See anything you like?" He asks again.

"Do you?"

"Definitely." His low, husky tone brings heat to my cheeks for all of two seconds before he smirks and pulls *Seduction for Dummies* from behind his back. "This."

A shiver slithers up my spine and I shake my head, "You should definitely read that."

"I guess I should." He flips through the pages and rests the half open book in his palm. "Strangely though, the first step is to catch a pirate."

We laugh too loudly and garner several angry looks. I stare at an old woman who obviously thinks we're in a library and not a busy airport bookstore, and eventually, she drops her eyes. I smile smugly at myself, relishing my small victory.

"What's her problem?" Seth whispers in my ear. He's suddenly very close, his hand brushes mine and goosebumps erupt across my skin. I ignore them as I tell him the story of Agnes, the decrepit old librarian who got kicked out of her job for misreading people, often giving them the wrong book, which in turn, up ended their lives in one way or another.

"She sounds like more of a witch than a librarian," he says.

"Some say she was. Now she roams airport bookshops and tries to re-live the glory days of shushing people."

"How about this one?" He hands me a book.

The light blue cover depicts two people holding hands. "What's it about?"

"Two people who go on a journey to find themselves." Our fingers graze as he hands me the book, and we look up at the same time. The hazy look in his eyes sends a strike of lightning inside my body. I feel like a school kid, butterflies fluttering in my stomach and buckling knees. It's ridiculous.

"Sounds great." I snatch the book away and step back, "What are you getting?"

"This one," he holds up *Tracking for Dummies.*

"Really?"

"Might help with my job."

"Well, you clearly need all the help you can get."

"Hey." He launches himself at me, and I shriek like an idiot. More glares and we both freeze, remembering the place is crawling with security guards.

We pay, and somewhere between putting our wallets back in our bags and walking out, Seth's hand lands on my shoulder and we run out giggling like two conspiring schoolgirls.

We take hurried steps away from the bookstore and meander down the duty-free isles.

"So, what does 'construction' actually mean?" My eyes snap to his toned muscular forearm.

"I'm a builder. My brothers and I own our own business."

"Brothers?"

"Yeah, one older and one younger."

"Are they better looking than you?" I smirk.

"No."

I giggle at his poor defense and don't miss the slight red tinge to his ears. "So, these less handsome brothers of yours, what do they do in the business?"

"Lachie is my older brother, he's a sparky, and Jake is a plumber."

"Sparky?"

"Electrician." He chuckles.

"You speak funny English,"

"It's cause we're making it better."

I nod to myself, wondering what else Seth could make better.

We wander around the duty-free killing time when we walk by a bridal shop. Two mannequins adorn the window, one wearing a splendid lacy wedding dress while her groom is dressed in a black, modern tuxedo with the top two buttons of the crisp white shirt open.

I stop to stare, mainly because I wonder why there's a bridal shop in an airport terminal. When I look up, I see my reflection framed perfectly by the veil and my body reflects the beautiful white dress. I catch Seth's eyes as they rake over my body and don't miss the way they grow and round just a little. I smirk and check my watch again, "We better head back."

He nods and I can feel his reluctance to do so, it mimics my own. Time with Seth has been more fun than I anticipated, and for the first time in a week, I haven't thought about her at all. I've eaten and laughed, and somehow, I feel like I've rejoined the living after a short stint gripped in the darkness of depression.

When the news came, I didn't take a single day off work. I didn't want to stop, cause stopping would give me too much time to think. I needed something to do, my hands to move and legs to walk and my brain to be full of other people's problems. Problems like when their orange juice was arriving, needing more cream in their coffee, wanting chicken instead of beef even though we've already run out, or that their tea is tasteless—though there's never anything to be done about that.

While I worked, I could plaster on a smile and be emotionless. I could push everything down during a twelve-hour leg. But as soon as the cabin lights went off and the passengers settled in, it was just me and the gaping wound of her loss. The absolute devastation. And then, as the lights turned back on, I had to fix my hair and makeup and convince myself that if I could keep it all together on the outside, I could do the same on the inside. I've been saving up my grief like a down payment for a house. It's full to the brim and about to burst, but soon it will all be spent in one large deposit—in Maya's arms as we say our farewells.

I don't even realize we're halfway to our gate when the ringing sing-song announcement tone blares above us.

"Passengers of flight SK98 to Phuket, please be advised your flight is boarding. Please make your way to the gate."

Seth and I exchange a melancholy look, like maybe he doesn't want his day to be over either.

All the passengers congregate at the gate. They mill around and line up, excitement once again seeping from their pores. We wait for twenty minutes before they announce a second delay. We find a place to sit and fall into easy conversation, checking the other passengers and making up the stories of their lives.

An hour later, one of the hostesses that's been waiting at the counter and speaking on a two-way radio picks up the microphone and the announcement tone rings above us again.

"All passengers of flight SK98 to Phuket please be advised this flight is now canceled and is rescheduled for tomorrow morning at 9 a.m., please see our staff at the SK counter to help you with..."

Passengers all stand at once and crowd the counter.

Raised voices and angry shouts fill the space while the air hostesses do their best to soothe everyone's irritation.

Seth and I remain seated We stare at the screen, waiting to see if perhaps there's been a mistake. The canceled strip glares back at us, red and angry.

"Fuck," I swear under my breath and Seth seems to share my sentiment. I check my watch. "Why did they leave it so late?"

"They obviously thought they could fix it."

My head snaps up and I glare into his eyes, "What did you do?"

"Well, I couldn't let any flights take off while my pirate bounty is still running free around this airport somewhere."

I chuckle then glare at him, "What about all the other people you stranded?"

"Fuck them, my bounty is worth way more."

I shake my head as we stand and make our way to the air hostess station. The two women look at us, their attention drawn to Seth. I can't blame them really.

"We're very sorry," they start and hold up some coloured vouchers, "here are your food and beverage coupons, which you can redeem at the food court any time until our sched-uled departure tomorrow." She hands them to Seth and I snatch them out of her hands.

"Thank you," I say with a singsong voice and a 'fuck you' smile. Seth plays along, throwing his arm around me and he gives them his most charming smile. My heart trips as Seth spins us around and leads us out and back towards the main duty-free area.

He doesn't remove his arm. It slips in neatly around my hip and rests there and I don't mind one bit.

"So, where's your ship? Maybe we can get out of here after all, pirate?"

"Not a pirate," I correct. "Down for repairs, it's why I've

had to settle for commercial aviation with the rest of the sheep."

"Baaaa," he calls out and a few heads turn to stare at us as I shove him playfully on his shoulder. I feel the flex of his arm around my hip to ensure he doesn't lose his grip on me. "So, no ship?"

"No."

"So where are you spending the night?"

I look around and spot an empty bench, "That looks comfortable."

His brow creases for a moment, and he shakes his head in mock disgust. "Too dangerous, pirate. You'll be totally exposed, and any bounty hunter could come and claim you as his prize."

"Still not a pirate, but I guess you have a point. What about you? Are you local? Do you have a place nearby?"

He seems to churn on the question for a moment, "No."

It's a short, curt answer, so I don't pry. But I've obviously touched a nerve.

"I have a proposal." He keeps walking pulling me along with him and away from the unoccupied bench, and I spot the bridal shop we walked by earlier.

His gaze follows mine as I answer, "Already? But we've only just met." He chuckles at my lame joke.

"How about a room at the airport hotel?"

"What sort of girl do you take me for?" I feign mock disgust even as heat shoots through my body.

"A *double* room." He's quick to correct and his words are like an ice bucket on the chemistry I've been feeling between us.

I think about my slim funds and the cost of our *'breakfast'*. Spending the day with Seth has been amazing. He's allowed me a reprieve from my overbearing sadness, a glimpse of joy. But spending the night with him might lead to more. A night where he might strip away my grief with his rough hands and beautiful smile and thick, full lips and strong body. I shake my head, batting the thought and the rush of heat away. "Thank you, kind sir, but I don't think I could afford it."

He keeps walking us toward the exit even as I speak, as if he didn't hear a single word I said. "Surely a pirate such as yourself has a hidden treasure somewhere?"

"Smuggler," I correct, "and if I did, it's buried very deep and very far away from here."

"Let's just go and ask how much they charge for a room."

I sigh and allow him to lead to me through the wide front doors of the airport and into the freezing night air. It's easy to forget how quickly the temperature changes here—hot one second, freezing the next. I shiver and he tightens his grip around me, sending a different sensation through my body. I like the way his touch is almost possessive. We make our way to the courtesy bus and stand in the shelter, waiting. It's open on one side and the light breeze bites at my skin. Seth doesn't seem phased by the cold at all, but his face crinkles as he studies mine.

"Cold?"

"A little," I lie through my teeth. *I'm bloody freezing.*

"Come here." He doesn't ask, just pulls me to him and cages me in his thick strong arms standing with his back to the wind, sheltering me. My gaze latches onto his and something passes between us—electric, dangerous, volatile. My stomach knits as his eyes turn a shade darker, and his arms tighten around me. His scent of clean laundry and musk envelope me and saturate my senses—senses that should not be thinking all these thoughts that spiral through me. But fuck it, I'm frayed and fragile and if a night with a stranger can help me cope, grieve, forget, then maybe I should allow myself to take that chance. She'd approve.

There's something about him that makes me want to melt into him, it's his easy laughter and easy-going nature. I'm drawn to him. His push and pull playfulness are part of his charm, and I'd be lying to myself if I pretend that I don't want to run my fingers along his torso and through his hair.

My eyes linger on the grand looking hotel across the road. I rest my head against Seth's hard chest, I'm grateful it's way out of both our budgets and I get to enjoy holding him for just a few more moments while we wait.

The bus finally arrives, and I hate detaching myself from his warmth while getting on. He slides in next to me and his arm automatically comes around my shoulder, pulling me to him as if it was expected, as if it's something we've always done.

Chapter Six

Abi

The short drive takes less than five minutes and we climb off and head inside. Seth spends no time looking around the rather drab lobby but walks us straight towards the reception desk tucked against the back wall.

I slip out of his grip and stop. He pauses and quirks an eyebrow in a silent question. "I just have to call Maya," I explain.

"Look, we've just met and it's been a long day, but I think I have it in me to satisfy you and a friend. I mean, I didn't think you were that sort of girl but if needs be, I'll be happy to—"

I elbow him hard enough to let him know he's not as funny as he thinks he is, but also soft enough to let him know that, if it comes to that, I don't feel like sharing him with anyone. I'm having too much fun. And I need it. *I need him.*

"My sister."

"Oh, right," he smirks. "I'll go ask about the room."

I nod and watch him walk away, wondering how his swagger got sexier in just a few hours. She would have landed in Phuket a few hours ago, her flight from Tel Aviv left the day before.

"Abi?"

"Hi." I automatically switch to Hebrew.

"Hi, what's going on? More delays?" She sounds annoyed. She always is when things are out of her control.

"They cancelled it altogether."

"Oh…" her disappointment warms me a little. We're not close. Mum brought us back together, like she always did. My heart constricts as the pain smashes into me.

"It's just a day. We will still have six more to do everything we planned."

"I know, I just wish you were here already." I can hear all the emotion well up in her voice and the quiver threatens to cut me open. Seth is walking back, and I need to end this call before I turn into a useless mess.

"Me too, but I'll see you tomorrow. I'll text you as soon as we've boarded."

"Ok." She says on a heavy sigh. *love you.*

"I love you too." I revert from Hebrew back to English just as Seth comes within earshot and our eyes meet. I hang up and put the phone back in my back pocket.

"It's a bit early for that," he winks.

His humor helps to balm some of the pain dredged up by Maya, and I give him a halfhearted smile. If he notices the change, he says nothing.

"I have good news and bad news." He starts.

"Ok…"

"Good news is they have room."

"And the bad news?"

"Only one room."

"And?"

"It's a standard room."

"Which means?"

"One double bed. But I can sleep on the floor," he throws in before I have anything to say about it.

"Seth–" I Feel like I should protest. After all, he wasn't going to let me sleep on a bench.

"I've slept on worse, plus I'll be safe with a pirate watching over me." He nudges me, and I can't help but smile.

"Smuggler," I correct and sigh. "Are you sure?"

"I've already paid for the room, so–"

"You what?"

Before he can answer, a bus load of Asian tourists walk into the lobby and make their way to the elevators. Seth grabs my hand and leads us in the same direction. His hand laces into mine and the charged heat between us is back.

∞

רציתי

∞

The tiny elevator fills up with bodies. We are cramped like shoppers at a Saturday morning flea market. The small space keeps filling until there is nowhere to go, and I find myself flush against Seth. My body hums with his warmth. His eyes find mine as the elevator jerks and moves, and as we ascend, we remain suspended in eye contact. The world falls silent as I fall deeper and deeper into his gaze.

His fingers trail down my arm and I inhale him, shutting my eyes. His chest rises and falls against mine in an uneven rhythm, and my body burns with heat. When I open my eyes again our faces are lined up and his lips brush mine, nothing but a whisper of a touch that echoes inside me. The sensation is like a lightning strike in a dry field, it sparks a hot burning flame inside me that spreads and catches under my skin.

He feels it too. I can tell by the way he stiffens for a second as he pulls away and his honey eyes turn a dark shade of whiskey. His hands slide around my waist and pull me tighter against him so that I can feel his hard muscles and massive erection.

My pulse riots beneath my skin. The air feels thicker as the elevator stops and we stand frozen, glued to one another as a few people step out. We continue our journey. His gaze locked on mine, asking the same questions that swirl inside me. Another stop and a few more people step out, and still, we are two statues—an unfinished work of art waiting to be molded, completed, uncertain as to what the artist has in mind for us. The elevator pings again and the doors fly open and the last of the passengers get out, and suddenly it's just Seth and me. It's like a switch has been flicked on and our bodies remember how to move. His hand plunges into my hair and his lips smash into mine in a punishing, needy kiss which heats my blood and fills me with reckless lust.

The elevator pings and the doors slide open. In a swift move, he grabs me by the hand and we're in the corridor where his body pins mine against the old wallpaper. The rough ridges dig into my shoulders. My hands tear down his back, fingers dig into his strong broad shoulders, and all I want is to feel the skin beneath. I reach for his belt and release the buckle. I suddenly want him inside me so badly, like his touch is the only thing that can quell this storm inside. His hand slithers up my shirt and slips under my bra, his rough thumb rolls over my nipple and I moan into his mouth.

A door creaks open somewhere, and he breaks our kiss. It's painful and I can see he's loath to release me. His hand closes around my wrist and he yanks me down the corridor, restless hungry eyes search numbers as we half run, half stumble.

"This one," his raw, breathless voice urges me on. And

then he's kissing me again, even as I fumble with the card key. The door flies open and I stagger back just to be caught in his strong arms. For a second the world spins, and then my body slams against the door, and his lips crush into mine, and his hands rip at my shirt, and my breath hitches in my throat, and I don't want any of it to stop or slow or end.

His lips work down my throat, and my head falls back against the door. The scruff on his chin leaving a hot, angry trail as he bites and nips at my neck.

His hands slide down to my ass and he lifts me with a powerful haul. My legs wrap around his hips like a belt, and he starts walking. He's kissing me again, or maybe still. Long drugging kisses, frantic and urgent and commanding my body to yield to his.

He sets me on the bed, smothering me with his body. His mouth unlatches from mine only long enough to rip his shirt away and tear at my bra. I get only seconds to admire his torso, wide athletic shoulders, sloping over his strong chest, and his abs, long and lean muscles that narrow at the waist and a deep carved V that arrows to his hard cock pressing against his jeans.

His dark gaze settles on me, and my stomach does a slow roll. Then his head dips and his mouth veers along my jaw, trailing lower still. His hot mouth closes around a nipple and I moan a shuddering sound that rips from my throat. His hands are everywhere as if ravenous. Rough, almost like fine-grit sandpaper, dexterous and skilled yet brutish and battered. My skin craves his weathered touch shaped by hard labour.

We fumble with our pants and underwear; and still we kiss and touch in a mad frenzy as if neither of us can get enough, consumed by madness, our urgency drives us on. His fingers drag along my body, my nails claw at his back, and we're a vortex of movement and hungry savage need.

He pulls closer, pressing my body against the length of his

till our faces are level for a second. His cock slides along my drenched pussy, long and thick and veined. I wrap my legs around his hips and rise to meet him. He's inside me in one stroke.

The muscles of his forearms flex as he holds himself above me. My gaze latches to his darkening eyes as he slams into me, hard and relentless like a storm, stealing my breath. I feel all my defenses melt away like salt in the rain, and before I can draw air into my body, I have molded into his form.

Pleasure crackles inside me, little sparks of electrical currents explode across my body. His low, ragged breaths permeate the air, as he keeps hammering into me. My hips roll up to meet him, needing more of his heat, of his relentless thrusting, of his warm body and bruising kisses.

He wrenches desperate moans from my mouth as he keeps hitting the right spot again, and again, and again. He lowers himself over me, his hands caging my body, the cords of his neck stretch taut, his lips latch onto my throat and his teeth drag along my skin.

Pleasure splinters across my body. "Fuck," I choke out as I come untethered and I grind into him, pulling him in deeper, harder, while he pumps a few more erratic strokes before he groans. His locked jaw ticks, his eyes screw shut and he stills inside me. His nails bite my skin, his teeth clamp down, his cock buries itself deeper. Everything about him seeks to be inside me and I want him to be.

We're undone. And for a moment, all I can hear are his frayed breaths and my thundering heart as it echoes back to me.

His mouth finds mine and kisses me. A long, deep kiss that melts whatever is left of my bones. Then he slowly raises himself up and slips out of me, rolling onto his back.

We lie for a few moments, catching our breaths, my mind

reeling, my heart ricocheting in my chest. Staring at the ceiling, exhilaration, disbelief, embarrassment all blend together to create a new sort of emotion that wells in my chest and sits waiting to be felt and dealt with.

He turns to look at me; his face flushed, his floppy hair tossed about in a wild frenzy, his lips swollen from kissing.

"That was…" he runs a hand into his hair as if searching for words. I feel the same.

"It was amazing." I reach for his hand and lace my fingers through his, "I never knew my first time would be this good."

The flush falls from his cheeks and his face crumbles like an old city wall. His eyes turn to saucers and his mouth falls open. He looks cartoonish as I fight hard to keep a straight face.

"You… were a virgin?" He can barely speak. The words come out choked and confused.

"I thought you knew, and that's why you proposed back in the terminal." I let my chin drop to my chest, "I thought it was obvious."

He snatches his hand away from mine, suddenly afraid to touch me, "What? No? That was amazing. But wait? You were really a virgin?"

"Yeah." I go in for a cuddle, and he backs away. I bite my tongue to stop my laughter, my teeth sink too deep into the flesh and tears spring to my eyes. He stops short.

"I mean… fuck. Abi, are you okay? Did I hurt you? I wasn't exactly…" he's out of the bed and pacing, his hand clutching the back of his neck. I watch his body move, realizing I didn't get a chance to appreciate it when we tore our clothes away. He's lean and tall, and his muscles flex and ripple—not muscles toned in a gym but earned on the back of his hard work. My gaze journeys slowly down, noting the stuttering of hair on his chest and the long thick line of hair that arrows from his navel down to his cock that swings semi erect between his legs. I like seeing him naked. He's lovely to look at, so lovely I've lost track of what he was saying. When I look back at his face, his jaw is taut and he's looking at me like he's expecting me to say something.

"Sorry what?" I fade back in, but only barely as my eyes keep slipping downwards.

He snatches a pillow from the bed covering his best parts and waits for me to look at his face. I pout and he zeros in on my mouth for a second, before holding my gaze, tender and endearing.

"Look Abi, that was incredible. But I'm sorry, I never should have... taken advantage. I just assum—"

"I wasn't good enough for you? Is that it?" I turn away from him so he doesn't see my creeping smile, the quiver in my voice and shudder that runs down my body as I fight off laughter only rattles him more.

"No, it's just that—"

"But I love you." I look directly in his eyes as I force mine as big and wide as I can get them, "Our wedding day will be the best day of my life."

"You what? Wedding..." whatever colour he has left trickles away like cold tea into a drain.

"I love you." I push myself up and bore into him.

He backs up, eyeing his jeans on the floor, and I know I can't keep this up much longer. "Erm, look Abi... you're obviously experiencing some strong feelings for me because you just lost your virginity to me. But—"

"Oh, I wasn't actually a virgin." I decide to let him off the hook.

He stops moving, his head tilts slightly to the side, and his brow furrows in deep groves, "What?"

"Come on Seth, how many pirate virgins do you know? What kind of bounty hunter are you?"

He stands there, his face still set in confusion, "So you're not a virgin then?"

"No." I don't bother hiding the massive grin on my face.

"And this wasn't your first time?"

"Of course not."

He shakes his head and I can see his shoulders drop, the tension leaking out slowly while my words sink.

"I can't believe you!" He growls before the pillow he's holding smacks my face. A second later he's on top of me, my hands in a vise grip over my head, his strong body shaking above me.

"That was evil."

"It's the pirate way." I wink at him and his mouth crashes into mine then just as brutally pulls away.

"Thought you said you were a smuggler? I should punish you."

"I'm a smuggler, I've endured all sorts of torture, not sure there's anything you can do that hasn't been done already." He groans at my words, and I bite down on my lower lip. His eyes flash with wicked intent and heat splinters inside me. *I can't wait to be punished by Seth.*

"You're going to drive me crazy," He says as his head dips down and his hot mouth latches around a nipple, lavishing it with attention. I moan and I know he's the one that's about to drive me crazy when a phone rings somewhere in the room.

Seth stops cold and the playfulness drains from his face. He releases me looking apologetic, "Sorry, I need to get that."

He pulls away from me and moves to the edge of the bed where he searches the floor for his discarded jeans. I can't help but follow him and grab his fine ass as he reaches down. He shoots me a devastating look before he reaches into the pocket and pulls out his phone. As he yanks it out, an object drops and rolls on the carpet. I go to grab it then stop short, my body freezing and my heart flailing.

Seth follows my gaze and suddenly his phone is forgotten as he snatches the engagement ring from the floor.

His fist clenches tightly around the ring and his mouth stretches into a tight, thin line. Fun, easy going Seth disappears in front of my eyes and turns into something hard and cold.

In a second, I'm out of the bed and reaching for the sheet. I cover myself and start scrambling, my head trying to wrap around what I've just done and what I've just seen.

"You're unbelievable," I hiss as I search for my clothes, which are scattered all over the floor as if a hurricane smashed through it. "I can't believe I'm so stupid."

"Abi." I'm sure it's his voice but the noise inside my head is unrelenting, like a freight train careening towards my ear drums.

"You're about to be engaged? Does she know you're a lowlife piece of shit?" I can't look at him.

I spot my underwear and reach for them, still clutching the sheet to my body as if it might protect me from the wave of emotion about to wash over me and drag me underneath it.

"Abi." He sounds a little closer.

"I'm so fucking stupid." I find my jeans and grab them, when his fingers curl around my arm and snatch me up, turning me to face him.

"Abi, it's not like that." His face is so grim my heart trips for a second before my anger burns the hesitation away, and I snatch my arm out of his grip.

"I know exactly what it's like." And I do. I've been burned like that before, and now he's made me into one of these women. The anger spreads to my hand and I shove him with all the force I can muster. He takes a few small steps back.

"You don't," his voice cracks around the edges and hacks through the noise in my head, "she left me."

His words are like a knife to my inflated balloon of fury, and as they pierce me, I feel the anger slowly fizzling out. "She left you?"

"Yes." He falls onto the edge of the bed and pulls the blanket over himself, resting his elbows on his knees his face sinks into his palms. His stark features soften with vulnerability and crease with pain.

Chapter Seven

Seth

It was going so well till Jess' ringtone caught me off guard and that fucking ring fell out of my pocket. Watching Abi's face collapse was almost as painful as watching Jess walk out of our apartment and close the door behind her. Now I've managed to fuck up twice in one day. For a second, I wonder what Jess wanted. Maybe she saw the walls. But then my thoughts drag back to Abi. It feels too soon to confess, to get real with her. It was so much fun being a bounty hunter and her being a pirate. It was simpler and less dangerous. But if I don't tell her everything, she'll leave—and I don't want her to. I can't remember the last time I've had so much fun in one day, laughed so hard and fucked so intensely. There's already something between us that's consuming and fiery.

She pins me with her glare.

"Her name is Jess… was… is." I sigh as Abi's face hardens. I'm not fixing this fast enough. "We broke up." I settle for the short, simple answer and hope that will be that.

"How long ago?"

I cringe, "This morning." Her face remains passive in a way that unnerves me.

"This morning?"

I nod, "She left me for someone else." My voice fights the raw emotion that's suddenly clenching my chest.

"Seth." Abi makes a move towards the bed, but I hold up my hand, unprepared for the onslaught of visceral pain and fury that's bubbling beneath my skin. I feel like I'm covered in ice, it's so cold my nerves are on fire.

"I was caught completely off guard," I start, and suddenly I feel the need to spew it all out, like these feelings are poison that's spreading through my body and I need to expel it before it's too late and I'm consumed. "We were together for two years, I thought she was the one." I try to breathe but my throat tightens. "I bought the ring three months ago, I kept waiting for the perfect moment, you know?"

Abi studies me, her beautiful features strained with pained emotion.

"The moment never came, and then this morning–" I grind my teeth and clench my fists, and my whole body hardens as the thought strangles me, "she strolls into the kitchen and tells me she's met someone else…" I let the words trail off.

"Did you fuck her?"

"What? No!"

"Was she fucking him?"

I grit my jaw and remain silent. Abi's mouth falls into a sad little 'O'. "It doesn't make a difference. She said they had a connection. He made her laugh; he made her feel seen." I slam my eyes shut battling with my inadequacies. "I guess she found an intimacy with him that I couldn't offer her, that went beyond the bedroom."

The silence lingers between us, dark and heavy like a widow's veil

Abi approaches the bed again and the mattress shifts as

she sits next to me, keeping a safe distance between us. "Is that why you're going to Thailand?"

I nod, "I need some distance to clear my head, to deal." I clear my throat.

Her hand finds my fist, and her long, delicate fingers trace my blanched knuckles till I release it and she laces her fingers through mine. It's such a simple gesture. And somehow so cruel in its simplicity, because she could just as easily take them away and leave me wallowing in my aloneness. My heart constricts with her small kindness I didn't realize I craved.

My gaze shifts to her face and our eyes lock, suspended in the harsh silence around us.

I force down my feelings of failure and incompetence and try to settle all the whirling thoughts that slosh around my head, wondering how Abi must see me now—as less. I suck in a long, steadying breath and try to chip through our cold silence. "What about you?"

Her eyes fall from mine, flitting about the room restlessly. Her soft features darken, etched by underlining sorrow she's managed to shove away for the last few hours. Her mouth falls open and snaps shut a few times, like maybe her words are lodged in her throat and she's trying to shake them free. Her lower lip begins to quiver and chocolate brown eyes gleam under the dim light.

She bites down on her lip, sealing the grief inside, and shakes her head like she's trying to hold back an avalanche of pain. I grip her and pull her against me, holding her smaller body which starts to shake. The first tear falls on my stomach and rolls slowly down till it hits the blanket that covers me and soaks into the fabric. Her hands wrap around me and she holds on, as if to dear life, as her tears shatter on my skin. An agonized sound falls from her lips as she sobs with such a rawness, I can feel my heart ripping with her pain.

I hold her, just like she held me, and let her cry till the sobs turn to sniffs and the shaking settles and her hand pushes me away.

"God, you must think I'm crazy," she mumbles. Her beautiful face is tear-streaked, her eyes red and puffy with her tears.

"I thought that hours ago, and you keep proving me right with every passing minute." I try for humor.

Her lips twitch for a second, and the pain behind her eyes lightens. She wipes her face in the sheet she's still clutching to her chest and sucks in a ragged breath. "My mum died," she blurts, and a single tear slides down her cheek.

I wait till her restless gaze finds mine and she finds the strength to talk again.

"It's like every time I say it out loud, I have to keep facing the fact that it's real." Her eyes burn with more unshed tears. "I'm meeting Maya, my sister, in Phuket so we can go scatter her."

Her sadness spreads over me and skates across my skin—the coldness, like sinking into a shallow pool—and I cannot begin to imagine the depths of her own ocean of pain. "What was she like?"

Her gaze snaps to me and the grief that dominated her features trickles away. "No one ever asks that."

I shrug, unsure what else to say.

"She was my whole world. My hero, my closest friend, my greatest supporter." A small smile creeps on her face, "She was also the only person I know that could flip on a whim, kiss you one second and curse at you the next. She had a big heart and temper that can scorch you, so you never wanted to piss her off. Most people that knew her said she was a little bit crazy."

"Well, now I know where you get it from," I blurt out without thinking and her smile widens just a fraction, and I think I'm not in as much trouble as I thought I might be.

"I hope so." Her smile falters. "I miss her so much." Her voice cracks with renewed heartache, and I reach for her hand, wrapping it in my own then pull her against me.

I wing a hand around her naked back, my fingers slither along her soft skin, her hot breath fans my chest. She lifts her head, tears prickle her eyes as they dart over my face before her hand brushes up my back and tickles my shoulder. She kisses my chest—a gentle graze of her lips—before she lands a second and a third, trailing a slow path along my collarbone and the column of my neck. The sheet around her torso falls away and her delicate body is flush against mine, her loose hair tickles my skin as her teeth graze my chin. Her fingers tangle in my hair before her lips seek mine and her tongue darts out past the seam of my lips.

My breath fogs my throat as she pulls away the blanket I used as a cover and straddles me. She pulls away, her eyes creased—not with uncertainty but with tenderness—and all I want is to take her pain away. Her hands ghost over my face, tracing my jaw and cheeks, then sink into my hair. Her lips skate over mine, a whisper of a touch, before she kisses me. Softly and delicately, like we're both made of glass. Her hands sift through my hair and I don't dare touch her while our lips are locked, and her body needs mine. We sink deeper into the kiss, hungrier. I break away, needing more of her.

My fingertips feather along her legs, and I delight in the clench of her thighs around me. I trace her round ass and her long back, tucking long tendrils of hair away from her neck, resisting the urge to curl them around my fist and tug.

I kiss and bite at her skin, needing to taste her, savor her, revere her. She arches her back in invitation and for the first time I notice the delicate freckle that sits just below the edge of her left nipple. I can't help but kiss it, then suck her nipple into my mouth, grazing it with my teeth. She moans, and her body begins to roll slowly over mine. Her hot, wet pussy sliding back and forth against my swollen, throbbing cock. I tease her nipples, lavishing each one with attention—delicate nips and bites and swirls of my tongue that rip grateful moans from her lips and send shivers to my desperate cock.

She kisses my neck and my mouth like she owns it. Like it's always been hers and she's always been mine. She pulls away grazing my bottom lip as she does then grips my cock. A choked groan escapes me as she guides me inside her. Her fingers dive into my hair and she begins to move above me. She's like water in my arms, fluid and effortless in her motions. She drags out each of her movements, pulling away till just my tip remains inside her then slams down into me, burying me deep inside her warmth as she clenches around me, chipping away at my sanity. My throat tightens as my breathing becomes more erratic, and still she punishes me with her hips and her pace.

"Abi…" my voice cracks and my fingers claw at her back; desperation crackles up my spine.

I put my hand between us, my thumb finding her clit as she rolls above me, grinding. Her chest to mine, her breath hot on my neck, her moans ripping from her and her relentless body rasps against my thumb till a shiver wracks up her body. A shredded cry rips from her lips and her pussy clenches so tight, my hands grip her ass and thrust. I bury myself deeper as my orgasm smashes inside me and I come hard and fast, her pussy drawing every last drop of cum from my cock.

We collapse onto the bed and find each other's lips between desperate gulps for air. When she releases me, her eyes remain latched onto mine.

She's all sweat and untamed just-fucked waves, her frame shaking with laboured breathing. Wrecked. I'm totally fucked.

Chapter Eight

Abi

Silence looms between us. It's thick and heavy like my desire for him. I feel equal parts stupid and powerful. Parts of me scream into the void of my soul, wondering how I jumped into bed with a stranger, while others push them over the edge and relish in the way he feels and tastes and makes me feel.

Even after I told him about eema, he didn't look at me with a hollowed pitying look like the rest of them. He looked at me like he wanted to eat me. Like he's been looking at me all day. Like he's looking at me now—with wild, uncertain eyes. The thought strangles me as awareness crackles beneath my skin. His full romantic lips curl into a smirk as I study his sharp jawline and high cheekbones.

"Like what you see?" He's all cocky and brash, his vulnerability swept away under the bed.

"I mean, I guess you're okay."

"I'm okay?" His eyebrows snap up, "You say that like you didn't just enjoy my company… twice."

My eyes rake down to where his groin is hidden beneath

the fold of the thin sheet. "No idea what you might be refer-ring to."

"Don't pretend like you weren't impressed," he shoots back, not missing a beat.

"What ever do you mean?"

He chokes out a laugh, "Would you like me to show you? Again?"

"You might have to," I purr into him.

One of his hands slides along my back and makes its way up into my hair, he fists the strands and tugs. "Till then?" He growls as he pulls me to him, our chests flush, and then his mouth consumes mine. The kiss is warm and strong and sensual and tender with a hint of all his rough edges. When he releases me, I feel lost.

When I open my eyes, his mischievous smirk paints his entire face, and I push away from him playfully, "You'll do."

"I'll do?"

I nod and suck on my lower lip, savoring his taste in my mouth and wondering what his cock tastes like.

His chuckle is a low grumble. He falls onto his back and pulls me to him. My head rests on his chest and his erratic heartbeat tumbles through me, mimicking my own. My fingers idly play with his chest hair and I breathe him in. He smells different now. Full of sweat and sex and me, and everything about him makes me want more.

"Hey, sorry about your mum." His voice is gentle and kind, not full of pity.

"It's ok," I whisper and swallow down my pain. Guilt suddenly floods my veins. "I don't usually do this, you know."

"This?" His voice is dipped with mock misunderstanding.

I slap his torso, a smile niggles at my lips, and pull my head away from his chest to look in his eyes, "You know what I mean."

"Do I?" He keeps feigning innocence.

"I don't pick up strange bounty hunters and take advantage of them in hotel rooms."

"You took advantage of me?" He pulls the sheet up to his chin, "I feel so used."

"Would you like me to use you again?"

"Fuck yes," he kisses me before reluctantly pulling away, "but I might need to have some food first."

"Good idea," I say as my body suddenly feels starved. "I can order us some room service. What should we have?"

"Well, I'm gonna have another burger. You can have a shot of rum, and we can work dessert out later."

∞

לנשק

∞

I wake up tangled in Seth and sheets. I don't feel like I've actually slept, but then I've never been much of a sleeper. My body feels stiff and heavy after using Seth's body to shield me from my pain.

I unwrap myself from him and watch him sleep for a while. My heart constricts with the well of emotion that opens inside me; guilt, lust and grief slosh at the bottom, and I don't know which emotion I'll drag up when I haul up my bucket. I should be mourning, instead I find myself falling. It sounds insane. I've barely known Seth for twelve hours and yet everything we've shared has been incredibly intense. I'm drawn to this man who, in such a short time, made me feel more alive than I have in years.

I shake off my crazy thoughts, putting them to our emotional states—the broken crevices in our hearts which need filling. We're both looking to be healed, and once we leave this hotel room…

I shrug off the sheets and head to the shower, where I'm loath to wash his smell from me. I know reality will come back soon and smack me in the face, and maybe I need to stop indulging in stupid fantasies and face the pain. Then again, Seth is naked in the next room and we still have a few hours to kill. I let the hot water crash against my skin while massaging my sore, angry muscles. I step out of the shower and wrap a towel around me before I go back into the other room.

Seth's hungry gaze rolls over my body, beads of water drip down my shoulders and seep into the towel. "Sorry, I didn't mean to wake you," I whisper even though he's awake.

"You didn't," he says lazily, "bounty hunters never really sleep."

"So, all that snoring last night was fake?"

He huffs, garbles something, and I can't help the loud snort that resounds somewhere in my nose and throat.

His eyes shoot to mine as heat branches across my face, "You're so sexy when you make those sounds."

"Says the man who sounded like a lawnmower last night."

"I can't help the noises I make when you're around." His voice is suddenly low and husky, and his hand reaches out and grabs my towel, jerking me to him. "Now," he purrs as the room whooshes and spins and my back lands on the soft bed, "I'd like to hear how you sound when I do this." He rips my towel open and sinks to his knees at the base of the bed, and before I have a chance to register what he's doing, his head dips and his whiskers scratch the inside of my thigh a second before his tongue lashes out. At the first flick he groans, and I think I might melt at the sound. He sounds hungry and delighted and god damn savage.

Seth pins me down with his strong hold. My eyes screw shut as he latches onto my clit, sucking and licking, ratcheting up the pleasure. My eyes fly open when he sinks two fingers into me and lock onto his as his soft mouth devours me. But that's the only thing that's soft about him. Everything else about him is hard—his darkening eyes, the swell of his biceps, the sloping shoulders. The way he kisses me down there is unrelenting, and my fists clutch the sheet around me, wanting to be locked around him instead, feeling his absence.

He takes mercy when I whimper and squirm, my head falling back, sinking into the soft bed, needing relief. He punishes me when he pulls away. I cry out in disappointment. A salacious smirk adorns his glistening lips.

But then he stands with his cock his hand, hard and veined as he strokes it. A droplet of pre cum leaks out, and I lick my lips remembering his flavour. He climbs onto the bed, pulling me back with him. His arms weave around me like restraints and his mouth smashes against mine. When he kisses me, he tastes like me… a little salty and a little sweet. He's hungry, insatiable, commanding and he glides smoothly inside me. Seth rocks against me, my hands shoot to his ass, the muscles flexing against my palm. Pleasure simmers inside me, my skin feels alive beneath him—wet, hot, chaotic. Like a storm. Pleasure washes over me, and I call out his name. I pull him deeper, harder, clenching around him. He groans, his neck cords and his arms tighten around me unyielding, constricting, and strong.

I feel safe.

Sated.

Spent.

I'm ruined.

∞

אותך

∞

Seth

I stab the fork into my eggs and chew on the overloaded mouthful, I'm starving. Abi has worked my body into such a frenzy that I'm famished, and even though I'm eating, I think I'm hungry for something entirely different.

Again.

I bat away the thoughts that keep derailing me and tune back to her words.

"...about four years now," she says between bites.

"And you enjoy it?"

"It has its ups and downs." She winks at me and my cock twitches in my pants.

"So, have you ever? You know..." I wiggle my eyebrows at her as I mime a plane taking off then create a circle with my thumb and index finger and push my other finger in and out through the middle a number of times while grunting and moaning. Her eyes grow wider for a second and her luscious lips turn up in a smile, and I can't help but remember them wrapped around my cock earlier. My balls tighten and I have to breathe out to release some of the building tension in my pants.

It doesn't help.

"Not yet," she winks at me and my jaw drops.

"Is that an invitation?" The sly smile that creeps across her face makes everything below my belly button tight and sets my mind on a tangent, "I'm going to take that as a yes."

I wait for the 'no', and when it doesn't come, I growl as I bite into my toast and Abi laughs at me. I don't care. I love her laugh; I love how her face lights up and her eyes shine, and that film of sadness evaporates off her.

I stop mid chew and examine my thoughts, specifically the ones which wonder what it would be like to always make her laugh. My jaw clenches as I think about Jess and how I used to feel the same about her. The thought is like a glacier over a volcano. The heat doesn't fade, instead it's like my mind is fogged with steam and heat and confusion.

I know I loved Jess, or at least I thought I did. Maybe it was always the idea of her. I don't want to draw comparisons, but it's inevitable. Jess was beautiful and kind, she liked to be seen and liked to be touched. But when I really delve and examine and prod our relationship, I know much of it never progressed past a certain point. We never evolved, we never found our real rhythm, we lived parallel to one another with different interests and friends; whereas Abi, in just twenty-four hours, challenges everything. Not taking any of my shit, giving it as good as she gets, and the way her body molds into mine is like she was made for me.

The rest of breakfast is spent on the little details, bits we missed asking one another in the last twenty-four hours. Not important earth-shattering revelations, but pieces that seem somehow relevant. We try to cram in as much as we can into our last hour together. I hate that Abi is already dressed and that both our bags are packed and waiting by the door.

I take her hand in mine as we walk out of the room and through the corridor. The walk feels much shorter than it did last night when we were trying to find the room. When her lips were locked with mine and her hands were ripping at my belt. I exhale deeply trying hard to quell the excitement building in my pants. I somehow have to survive an eight-hour flight.

We take the courtesy bus back to the terminal with Abi tucked against me. Shit, she fits perfectly into the crook of my arm. I hate having to release her when the bus stops and we have to climb off.

We're hovering in a strange space, somewhere between

apprehension and happiness. An uncharted territory that has us walking slower and remaining silent. When we get to that gate, when we board that plane, when we go our separate ways, it will all be over. Yet, this delicate, wonderful, and strange thing between us feels like it should be allowed to grow and develop—that we should explore it. We're both too scared to ask the question. It's too soon, it's too insane.

We sit at the gate and somehow manage to maneuver out of the land of uncertainty and back to a place where Abi is a beautiful woman at an airport and I'm the guy that got to make her laugh; and I do for the next thirty minutes while we wait to board.

When we stand, she slides her fingers into mine like it's the most natural thing in the world to do, and the small gesture floods me with unwarranted happiness. Fuck, this woman has me twisted in all the wrong angles. We shuffle along the queue, holding our passports and boarding tickets in hand, when Abi pushes on her tiptoes so that her mouth nears my ear.

"You know that thing that you asked me about over breakfast?"

"Which one? There were so many." *So many.* I chuckle as I think of the endless rain of questions that we battered at one another.

"You know…" She mimics an airplane taking off a single brow arches as she cocks her head to the side slightly.

My body somehow tries to inhale and exhale at the same time, and I choke as she smirks at me. I clear my throat, "Yeah, I remember, what about it?"

"I have an idea…"

Chapter Nine

Abi

"I can't believe you!" I cry a little too loudly, swivel in my chair and give Seth a scalding look. My chair vibrates with the movement. It's enough to draw a few eyes.

"What now?" He's part defensive, part nonchalance as he reaches over to touch my shoulder.

I jump out of my seat and narrow my eyes at him. "One of your girlfriends just sent me a message." I'm pretty sure the pilot heard me, as I stuff my phone in his face. He quirks an eyebrow. It's the best I could come up with. "As soon as this plane lands, I'm calling my lawyer!"

"Oh babe, I can explain." He stands and follows me down the aisle as I stomp off towards the bathroom, "She's a candidate to be our surrogate, you know how long we've been looking."

Asshole.

"That picture did not come from the agency! You're fucking her, aren't you? Just like you did the other two 'surrogates.'" I don't look back as I make my way down the aisle, watching the other passengers squirm in their seats, looking anywhere but at me. The silence behind me tells me Seth is hot on my trail.

"We weren't having any luck with that agency babe. I was trying something new, I wanted to do this for us."

"No. You wanted to try something new for you. What happened? Grow tired of the last one?"

"That's not fair, I was trying to do something nice for you."

"You could have asked me first!" I scream in his face then shut the bathroom door, locking it behind me. I cringe and suck in a deep breath wondering if I've gone a little overboard. I shrug to the tiny room. Probably.

"You've been so stressed with all of this babe, I wanted to help," he speaks through the door.

"You're the one that's been stressing me out with all your secrets and lies." I bite my smile down as I lean against the door.

"We need to talk about this." He's a little calmer.

"No!" I slam the door and am rewarded with the murmured voices of the air hostess hoping to moderate and pacify us.

"Abi, let me in. You know you can't hide in there for the rest of the flight, let's talk about this!"

I lean against the door and screw my eyes shut, asking myself for the millionth time since I stood up what the hell I was doing.

"Open the door, babe." There's no sweetness in his voice as his hand slams on the other end sending ripples through my body.

I suck in a steading breath and my trembling fingers unlatch the lock. I pull the door in just a little and find Seth standing at the entrance, his beautiful face twisted with heavy emotion. Two air hostesses are standing behind him, their eyes dart to me in silent questions.

"Come on Abi, let me in." His voice is suddenly honey and

low, and something happens low in my belly. *Damn he's good.* "Let's talk about it."

"Fine!" I growl at him and open the door all the way, allowing him to walk in and seal it behind him.

"You don't need to call a lawyer babe," he says a little too loudly as he pins me against the bathroom wall.

"Don't tell me what I need Seth." I snarl before his mouth finds mine and devours me in a hungry kiss. I can feel how fucking hard he is, his big cock strains against his jeans, and I don't feel the least bit guilty about spending the last twenty minutes stroking him in his seat.

"Be reasonable babe, I'm trying to do the right thing." He strains as I release his cock, and he pulls up my skirt and pushes my G-string aside.

"You're a cheating piece of shit."

The tip of his cock sits at my entrance, and he starts to thrust shallow and slow. "Fuck Abi," he strains.

"No!" I dig my fingers into his back, reminding him where he is and what we're doing.

"Just tell me what you want me to do," he growls and thrusts at the same time, sliding into me fully. I bite my lip keeping my moan sealed inside.

"Let me be the one who picks the other woman." I whine as he moves inside me.

"I will." He sounds tormented as he says the words and thrusts in again, and I just hope that we sound like a love-struck couple. "I didn't touch any of them, I swear."

"I don't believe you," I wail in a long torturous sound as his hips start to hammer into me.

Our bodies collide in the small stall and he holds us as best he can while his hips piston into me.

"This time is different." He barely manages as his grip on me tightens, his fingers digging into the flesh of my ass.

"I can't go on like this," I cry out and hope it sounds more angry than desperate as his unrelenting cock hits that perfect spot and pleasure threatened to overwhelm me.

For a second, his gaze locks onto mine. His honey eyes melt into my chocolate brown ones, and I know he understands.

"Me either, babe," he chokes out as he thrusts into me again, and I explode around him. My head whips back and my hands flex, automatically searching for something to latch on to, drawing him into me so that I can bite his shoulder and mute my moans. He jerks and stills for a second and I can feel his orgasm, I clench as he thrusts a final time and my body hums with heat and pleasure.

He draws in a long breath, his forehead glued to mine. "Is this it?" He sounds drained, but his smile is wicked and delicious.

"I guess so." I'm more breathy than angry. It doesn't even matter now.

He smirks as he sets me down.

"That was amazing," he whispers and steals a long, dizzying kiss that has my knees wobbling again. His hulking shape folds and twists in the confined space as he grabs a few tissues from the dispenser. He bends uncomfortably, and with a few long and gentle strokes, cleans the cum that now streaks down my inner thigh.

A knock on the door sends a volt of nerves through my body and has my heart kicking back up. "Is everything okay in there?" A female voice seeps through the door. A combination of curiosity and anger.

I pull down my skirt while Seth tucks himself back in, then I splash some water on my flushed face.

There's a second knock on the door, more insistent that time, "Sir, miss, I insist you come out right this ins—"

Seth unlatches the door and hangs his head. "It's over anyway," he snaps as he nudges past her and her eyes fly to me.

"I'm so sorry miss, it just sounded… we just thought…"

"I'm sorry." I bite my lip, holding in the ridiculous happy grin that wants to escape. "It's been on the cards for so long…"

She looks around at the full cabin. "I'm sorry. Our flight is full, I can't offer you another seat."

I sniff and suck in a breath, still coming down from my high, "It's fine, we're done now. Thank you though."

Her mouth draws into a thin line and she nods as I round her and make my way to my seat next to Seth—where he's sitting frowning and glowering like every male ever scorned.

He turns his head slightly and sneaks a devastating wink in my direction just as I sit down, and I bite down the smile that threatens to burst into my face. His knuckles graze stealthily along my thigh and I shiver at the touch, remembering how his fingers felt inside of me last night. Heat blooms beneath my skin as I squeeze my thighs together. When I looked up, I find Seth watching me squirm in my seat. His devilish gaze is hellfire, and at any moment I could burst into flame.

"Good morning ladies and gentlemen, this is your captain speaking. We've begun our descent to Phuket…" The captain continues with the usual spiel. I unlatch my eyes from Seth and focus on a spot on the aisle where the carpet is scuffed. I keep watching it till we touch down.

∞

כמו

∞

Seth

We disembark and the other passengers' eyes still bore into us. We have to keep the charade going, so our faces are set in annoyed scowls, which we shake off as soon as we put enough distance between us and the flight crew.

We make our way to baggage claim and stand at the carousel waiting for our bags. A strange silence hums between us, like a long favourite song coming to an end—we can both feel it.

"That one is mine." She darts forward and grabs a small compact suitcase. As soon as it hits the floor, she extends the handle and it rests at an angle on its wheels.

We stare at one another. So many words hanging over us, I feel like we still have so much more to say, to share, to laugh about. Letting her go now feels like tearing a fresh new wound on my already bleeding heart.

"I don't want you to go…","I had fun…" we say at the same time and smile.

"It was nice meeting you, bounty hunter."

"You too, Pirate." I wink at her, and she turns and starts walking away.

"Where are you staying?" I ask, desperation leaks into my voice.

"If you're as good a bounty hunter as you say you are, you'll find me." She winks at me.

"Really?" My voice is loaded with too many emotions to count. This isn't how it ends; she doesn't get to walk away, and we both know my bounty hunting skills need some work.

She laughs and comes back, throwing herself at me. Her lips catch mine, and the fire from earlier catches and flares around my skin. Her mouth, her body, her smile all get me turned on like a leaking faucet that I don't want to fix.

She takes out a piece of paper from her back pocket, her name and number written clearly in blue pen including little smiley face sporting an eye patch at the corner. She makes a show of folding it before her hands run down my back and into the back pocket of my jeans, where she squeezes my ass.

She kisses me again, long and deep and tender, and I know it's a goodbye kiss as she pulls away.

"Call me."

"I will." I watch her go even as my fingers reach for the paper and my chest expands with joy.

I unfold the torn shard of paper, grab my phone, and dial the number.

Abi stops mid walk, looks at her phone then swipes. A second later her perplexed sweet voice comes through the other end. "Hello?"

"Just checking," I say. She swivels towards me. I wave and smile. "Pirates have been known to play dirty tricks before."

"Smuggler," she corrects, and her face splits into a stunning smile before she hangs up, turns back around, and disappears behind the doors of the welcome area.

My breath leaves me. Relief and disappointment stir inside me as I return to the carousel and grab my bag. It suddenly feels a lot heavier.

Chapter Ten

Abi

I look at the smiling faces crowding the arrivals area and search for Maya. My heart leaps for a second as I see my mother just to realize it's Maya. They look so much alike, it's like being stabbed. I wonder if she feels the same looking into the mirror each day.

She waits for me as I run into her arms.

"Abi." She blows out my name as I push the breath from her body with a leap. Her warmth envelopes me as she tightens her grip around me, and I wrap myself around her.

She feels like home.

She feels so familiar that stupid, happy/sad tears prickle my eyes.

She releases me first, "Ready?"

I nod. She grabs my suitcase and starts leading the way to the exit. I feel a pang of guilt as I turn around hoping to spot Seth's sexy smile before we leave. I know I should be relieved not to find it. Still, my stomach drops in disappointment. Maya starts talking about a taxi and our hotel, and I know I should make an effort to embrace this time I have with her.

We're so different, and sometimes I get the feeling she doesn't like me as much as I love her.

Maya is a planner. Bold, ambitious, and beautiful, she plans everything down to the very last detail and always makes things perfect. She chases perfection like a drug. As kids, I used to follow her around and ask her to play with me. I wanted to run in the mud and look for slugs, she wanted to play mums and dads. I never saw the appeal, but I played along to appease her. She didn't reciprocate. She'd shoo me away when I came too close to her dolls with my muddy feet and my dirty face. She would wave her hands and scream as if I were a mosquito or some kind of ferocious animal.

When we grew up, we drifted even more. She was a straight A student that followed all the rules. She made all the right friends and kissed all the right boys. She was always so practical and logical and never driven by her emotions.

But me?

I was the one who cut school and spent weekends in venues I shouldn't have even been allowed into. My friends were the rejects and the freaks, and I kissed all the frogs, looking for my prince. But I was okay with all that, because I didn't want to live my life like Maya. I didn't want borders and rules and a box to fit into. I wanted to colour outside the lines, I wanted to splash colour everywhere.

As adults, we barely see each other. My job takes me away from home and family while she spends time building hers. I miss my niece and nephew, their sweet giggles and beautiful hugs, but the call of travel and adventure always ran hotter inside me. Like mum. She never sat still, and I know parts of her died a little when she stayed home for years taking care of us. I've never seen her freer or happier than when she grew her wings back and took off.

We step out of the terminal and the humidity hits me like a sledgehammer. It's like walking into a thick wall of hot water that slides around me, coating me in my own sweat.

A long line of taxis stretches on the road just outside the terminal, like a lazy yellow snake basking in the hot sun. The drivers wave and shout, each offering us a lift. I follow Maya blindly, knowing she would have already worked out where to go and how to get there.

It's so strange to be here with her. Though they look identical, she's the polar opposite of eema, with her stringent routines and perfect plans and schedules. It's no wonder they clashed so much.

We find a taxi and the driver throws my bags into the boot before slamming it shut and starting the car. Loud Thai music blares through the radio and the air con fights the humidity in a losing battle.

"I can't believe we're here." She sounds more melancholy than excited.

I clutch Maya's hand and squeeze. When she doesn't reciprocate, I draw my hand away and tuck it between my thighs. "Yeah." Is all I can muster as I gaze out the window and watch the view unfold before me.

The car veers away from the airport and disappears behind a dense screen of green vegetation. We drive over the black, winding road carved through the once thick forest. Homes litter the shoulder of the road; kids play, women chat and clothes flap in the breeze. The taxi climbs atop a hill, and as we begin our descent, my breath stalls as I get my first glimpse of Patong Beach beneath us.

The intense aquamarine of the sea sparkles along a seemingly infinite golden sandbar that stretches endlessly and hugs the edges of the island. People crowd the beaches like tiny ants. As we close in on the main town, the sea hides behind hundreds of stalls lined along the roadside, tourists shelling out their money on food and souvenirs. While the other side of the road is back to back shiny resorts, bars and restaurants all claiming to be the best. The road is congested with traffic—motorcycles, tuk tuks, taxis and pedestrians all fight for space to move about. Music, voices, and the distinct smell of suntan lotion all drift into the car.

I'm glued to my window. The mayhem drawing my attention, my eyes flinging from one thing to the next like I'm watching a ball bounce about in a pinball machine.

Our car comes to a stop outside a resort and Maya hands the driver a few notes. He climbs out, grabs my bags from the boot and hands them to a man in uniform who takes them and scuttles inside. A moment later, we follow and enter the beautifully decorated lobby. Greenery and wood and modern design all clash into one, and I make my way to the desk where a petite woman with a perfect smile and pressed uniform greets me and checks me in.

Maya leads us to our bungalow, and I want to squeal as I step inside an airy room to a stunning wooden deck overlooking the road. Somewhere beyond, I know there's the sea. There're two single beds pushed against the back wall. I drop my bags and sit on the edge of the one closest to the deck, knowing Maya would want to be near the bathroom, and fall backwards. I sink into the fluffy blanket and sigh.

"It's beautiful." I smile and catch Maya's half nod. My smile dissolves and I push myself up on my elbows, "We're allowed to enjoy ourselves—a little."

"I know." Her lips purse into a thin line and her gaze shoots across the room. I follow it and see what she's looking at. Any shred of joy I may have felt melts away like ice in the sun. eema's urn sits next to the TV; a plain black container that shows none of her personality yet holds all her ashes inside.

Emotion clogs my throat as tears spring to my eyes. I brush them away before they escape. "This isn't what she would have wanted, and this isn't how we planned it," my voice croaks.

Maya nods, "I know, but it's so hard to 'celebrate' her life when she's so dead."

A long silence descends on the room. I drag in a heavy breath; it's tinged with the raw salty taste of the sea that lies across the road. I jump from my bed and snatch my suitcase. "Come on! We're going to go and have fun, just like we said we would, just like she'd want us to."

I don't wait for a response, just start digging into my suitcase. I take out my bikini and throw off my shirt. I find a small bruise beginning to form along the rim of my hip where Seth held me down. Heat floods my body and I squeeze my thighs together, suddenly painfully aware of how much I miss him touching me there. *Everywhere.*

I chuck on my bikini and wrap myself in a sarong then find a faded Metallica T-shirt to finish the look. I'm done in less than five minutes and watch my older sister in fascination. She slips into a sundress and dons a large wide brimmed hat and oversized sunglasses before collecting our room key, suntan lotion, two bottles of water and a number of other items, shoving them all into a bag. She looks around the room like she's wondering if she can fit a kitchen sink into the bag before nodding to herself and running her eyes over me. She purses her lips but manages to say nothing, instead reaching for the urn. She tucks it under her arm and looks at me, "Ready."

"Are we really going to—"

"She's coming."

"Okay." I don't argue. I've been down that rabbit hole before. Maya will spin any story a hundred different ways to suit her needs till she wins an argument, going to unreasonable lengths to disprove indisputable facts.

The heat smothers me as soon as we leave the room. We walk through the lobby and out into the streets. I don't know where to look first, this place is a visual feast that can drown the unprepared. Maya slides her hand into mine and forges ahead. As long as she knows where we're going, I get to look around. We slice through crowded streets. Tourists and locals mingle in a multi-coloured rainbow, and the distinct scent of chili paste and fish permeate the air. We cross a busy street and then my feet sink into golden sand.

I freeze for a second, look at the beach and breathe when I finally spot the sea. It peaks beyond the countless deckchairs and people who bury the golden blanket with their presence—like they've been vomited on the beach and are yet to be washed away. I shake my feet out of my slip slops and follow Maya towards the water line. She pays for some chairs, drops her bag and eema into the sand, then gets comfortable.

"Are you coming?" She looks at me like she always does, like I've said or done the wrong thing. I shake my head at her, throw off my sarong and shirt and bolt towards the water.

My feet kick up sand as I sprint across the beach and run right into the lukewarm water. I plunge into the water and let it wash over me. Its calming effect is instantaneous, it soothes all my worries and anxieties as it always had. The waters feed my soul. I lay on my back letting the small waves lap against my face and the sun to warm my skin and the water to drown away all the noise around me, allowing memories to flood in.

A childhood spent under the sun where we guzzled cold watermelon and grapes coated in sand and sea water. Where we built castles and looked for shells. Sadness tries to filter itself into me, but I push it away. I think of my mother's face, of her rolling laughter and leathery skin, and I find joy in those memories. My body sinks and I go under, as my feet find the sandbar and I stand, I am filled with a new determination to make some new ones with my sister who feels too much like a stranger.

Water runs down my body in glistening rivulets, and I spot Maya lying on her deck chair. I sigh, dragging myself out of the water and plop into the chair next to her. She gives me a tight smile then digs a book from her bag and reads, leaving me to look around. I find myself searching faces and wondering where Seth might be and what he might be doing. I spend the rest of the morning soaking up the sun and feeling disappointed when I don't find Seth.

Chapter Eleven

Abi

The rest of the day is a daze.

Eating street food and baking in the sun, cooling down in bars with smoothies spiked with vodka, and a late dinner comprised mainly of rice and meat I'm inclined to believe is chicken. Maya thaws over the day but is still pensive and hard. She's still the same thick wooden door I've knocked at my whole childhood.

After dinner we go up to the room. Maya slides into the bed and grabs her book. I'm about to ask her if she'll mind whether I put the TV on, when my phone rings.

"Hello?"

"Pirate."

"Bounty hunter?" My heart beats a little faster at the sound of his voice and a stupid grin stretches across my face.

"Did you miss me?"

Desperately. "No."

"Ouch," he hisses, "that hurt more than realizing I wasn't the man who took your virginity."

I laugh at him, then clear my throat when Maya shoots

me a long glare, one of her eyebrows flying up to her hair-line. I step out to the balcony, "That does sound painful."

"Well, I know something that can soothe that pain?"

"What might that be?"

"A drink?"

"Where?"

"At your hotel bar."

My heart forgets its normal beat and slams erratically in my chest, knowing Seth is just a few walls away from me. "I'll think about it."

I hang up and run back through the room and into the bathroom. My skin is glowing from the sun and my hair is a frizzy mess tangled by the humidity. I splash water on my face and run it through my hair, hoping to tame some of the wild flyways and strands. I grab a black pencil and draw a long black line beneath each eye, smell my armpits, and slosh some mouthwash in my mouth. When I'm done, I grab my bag and turn to Maya.

"It's a bit early, I think I might go for a quick drink. "

She narrows her eyes at me and looks at her bedside clock. "Don't be back too late, we have that island trip booked for tomorrow."

"Don't worry, I'll be back soon."

She nods and her jaw wobbles for a second.

"Hey are you okay? I could stay—"

"No, don't be silly, go. I'm fine."

We share a long look and when she dips her eyes back to her book, I leave the room stopping myself from running full pelt to the bar.

I spot him sitting at the bar, nursing a beer. He's mid conversation with the barman. They burst out laughing and Seth's laugh booms across the room. He seems so at ease, or maybe it's just how his skin seems darker under the lights and his white T shirt shows off his muscular arms.

I inch closer to the bar and make sure to sit two stools

away. The barman sees me and excuses himself. I look straight ahead.

"What can I get you?" The barman asks in a heavy accent.

"She'll have a shot of rum." Seth's voice carries across the small distance between us. The barman's eyes jump from me to Seth and back again.

"Make it a Mai Tai," I say as I turn to look at Seth, "and put it on his tab."

"I see you're still taking every opportunity to take advantage of me." He slides onto the next bar stool, keeping one between us.

"Well, I did give you the most precious gift a woman can give a man."

"A blowjob?" He smirks.

I feel heat coat my body as I think about his cock in my mouth. I bring my hand to my mouth and gasp in mock horror, "My virginity!" I gape at him with an open mouth, while his stretches into a sexy smile that looks like he's either laughing at me on the inside or thinking about dirty deeds done behind closed doors.

He slips into the chair next to mine, "I enjoyed both equally." He winks at me and my heart skips, my insides turning into a warm puddle, but before I can melt, the barman puts my drink down.

I reach for it and take a long, hard sip, feeling Seth's eyes on my mouth.

"Did you have a good day?" he asks.

"It was… nice."

"Nice?"

"Could have been better."

"If you were spending it with someone else?"

I shrug and a slow, sly smile curves his lips.

"Didn't think you were the clingy type," he quips. "Anyway, I thought you'd like to spend some uninterrupted time with your sister."

He was being thoughtful. And I'm NOT clingy, but maybe I did miss his smile, and maybe his ass, and maybe the way I feel when we share the same space.

"I just meant I would have liked to be here under different circumstances. But sure, why not make it all about you?" I wipe the smile from his face and battle my own. He doesn't get to call me clingy and get away with it.

"So, this has nothing to do with running from a bounty hunter?" He doesn't take the bait and I like it.

"I don't run, I fight."

"Not very hard."

"Hey," I jab him with my elbow and heat sneaks up my arm at the feel of his skin, "you haven't seen my best moves."

Something flashes behind his eyes. "I bet," he says and licks his lower lip like he's thinking about them, making shivers travel down my spine.

I sip on my drink, trying to cool down the warmth that's rising inside me. Being around Seth has that effect on me, and he barely touched me, hasn't even kissed me—we're both holding back, building the anticipation, letting it claw at out skins.

He downs his beer and slams the empty glass on the bar, "Want to get out of here?"

"What did you have in mind?"

"Somewhere where I can see some more of your moves." His voice drops a few octaves, and my stomach drops with it.

"I don't know if you're ready for more of my moves."

"Guess we'll find out, pirate."

"Smuggler," I correct and suck down the rest of my Mai Tai. I slide off my seat and sashay towards the exit, then throw my head over my shoulder, my eyes locking on Seth's, "Do your worst, bounty hunter."

Chapter Twelve

Abi

"What are we doing here?" I shout at him, trying to be heard over the loud music thumping in the club. Seth drags us to the bar where he locks me in his arms, caging me in front of him and signals to a barman.

"I'm going to check out your moves," he calls out, his breath ruffles my hair, and I feel his smile over my shoulder.

He orders our drinks, his body grazes mine with the beat, teasing me with his proximity while never closing the distance between us, making my synapses jump like beans in a tin.

Six shots of green liquid drop in front of us and Seth hands the barman a few notes before grabbing his first shot. He waits for me to raise mine, and after the clink, he throws his head back and the liquid disappears. I follow his lead, downing all three shots one after the other in quick succession.

The alcohol scratches my throat and burns my stomach as it hits it with a resounding hot surge. Seth grabs my arm and pulls me to the packed dance floor. The place is electric. Everyone around us feeds off the music, smiling and dancing. The alcohol hits my blood stream like I've been tapped into an IV, and I start to move, my body swaying like it belongs to the music.

I dance, the music moves me like I'm a puppet on strings, my mind buzzes with joy, my worries and anxieties fall away, and nothing matters. Or maybe it's the alcohol. But it still doesn't matter, I'm happy.

There's so much sweat on my skin and not all of it is mine. Seth's slick body is glued to mine, his hands on my hips, his hot breath fanning my shoulder as we move to the beat as one. He feels perfect against me, and I know that later he'll feel just as good inside me. Sweat coats my forehead and my hair sticks to my scalp while we dance and move. I'm having fun again while Maya sleeps and laments in our room. I push the thought down with another sip of alcohol and feel Seth's lips close on that spot where my shoulder and neck meet, sending shivers across my body.

"Want to get out of here?" he shouts over the music.

I spin around and sling my hands around his neck, and when he looks down at me, everything else stops. His scorching stare cements me in his arms and desire pulls at every inch of my skin. His rough hands glide up my back and sink into my hair. Heat pools in my belly as he brings his lips to mine.

He kisses me like he's drowning and I'm his oxygen.

∞

שרציתי

∞

In the charcoal sky of almost-dawn, I walk briskly back through the lobby.

I turn the doorknob as quietly as I can, my eyes burning and bleary from alcohol and lack of sleep. I can't believe I have to be up soon and spend the day on a boat, when I'd much rather spend it rocking under Seth's body. My stomach lurches at the idea of rocking, and I drag in a long breath to settle it.

I sneak into the room, finding Maya awake and sipping a coffee on the deck. She tosses a long, angry glare at my direction, and I roll my eyes. It's like she thinks she's eema. Except that eema wouldn't have cared.

"Nice of you to come back."

"Don't start. I'm here aren't I?"

"Are you?"

"What's that supposed to mean?"

"It means every time I look at you, it's like you're looking to be somewhere else… or maybe with someone else?"

She's not wrong but I'm too tired and slightly tipsy to be having this conversation right now. I could tell her it's my grieving process, but that would be cruel and unfair. So, I bite my tongue and go over to her and throw my arms around her shoulders.

She wrinkles her nose and I don't blame her. I stink of alcohol, smoke, sweat and sex, "I know why we're here, but as much as we're sad, you know she'd want us to have fun."

She nods and pushes away from me. She's even more distant than usual. But I'll have to dissect that nut later. Right now, I need some sleep.

"How long till breakfast?"

"A couple of hours," she murmurs into her cup, and I nod as I land headfirst into my bed and the world fades away.

Chapter Thirteen

Abi

Two hours later, Maya drags me from the bed and forces me into the shower before we head for breakfast. She's quiet and sour as we drink our coffee and fill up on the continental breakfast. The grease coats my belly and helps to soak up a little of the alcohol from the night before. I develop a new appreciation for crispy bacon.

When we're done, we're herded outside and wait in the sun with a group of other guests. They're all excited and loud. My head wants to explode, and my eyes burn. All I want is a bed. *His* bed. I groan as the bus pulls up and the hotel is left behind me. I take solace in the air con and the soft seat I can rest my thumping head against.

The scuffed wooden pier sways a little under my feet, or that could be my unsteady legs as I follow the chattering crowd to our waiting boat—a long white vessel with plastic chairs sporadically bolted to its floor, beneath a metal roof. I look wistfully across the way at a speed boat docked further along the pier; the one with three brand new looking engines, enclosed cabin and tinted windows. I grimace before I clutch the damp, rusty ladder and climb aboard. It rocks and wobbles beneath me, and even after a full breakfast, my stomach lurches with every slight bob. I regret eating that second baguette.

I follow Maya to the back of the boat where we settle in for our trip. And by settle in, I mean she ignores me and glares over the turquoise water while I shut my eyes, and picture Seth and all the moves I showed him last night. A smile niggles at my lips as my head falls back against the plastic chair and lolls about. The rest of our group disperses and find a seat. The engine purrs to life and we lurch away from the mainland and over the sea. The boat skips and hops over the light waves, a light spray of water rains on us, cooling me from the scorching sun.

We fly by towering rocks that spear the earth, coated with greenery that hangs off the peaks like wild, dreaded wigs. Maya holds on to her bag of wonders, and I wonder if she has something for a hangover hidden inside. I didn't even drink that much. I should try and talk to her. I don't.

The boat drops its anchor a few hundred meters from our island destination. It's obscured by two colossal limestone rock giants that block our path. The captain explains we must make the rest of the way onto the island ourselves and offers us the option to snorkel or kayak. I don't wait to ask Maya what she wants. There's no way I'm swimming over while my skull feels like it's squeezing my brain.

We climb into the flimsy kayak; it rocks beneath us unsteadily. Maya clutches her bag between her knees, keeping it safe from the sloshing water on the red plastic bottom and grabs an oar, holding it awkwardly.

I let her do most of the work as I gaze at the striking limestone island. We meander through the two hulking rocks that tower above us like giant sentinels. They are the keepers of this place, and a light chill plays on my skin as we fall under their shadow. Maya expertly manoeuvres us between the two peaks, and we exit to find a pristine white sandy beach that kisses the crystal blue water.

We dock at the beach and leave our kayak with the others lining the beach. People mill around, some off exploring, others basking in the sunshine.

I turn to my sister and follow her gaze. She studies the raised peak covered in wild, dense vegetation. Her face set in a weird determination.

"I think this is it." Her eyes lock on mine and her words spear my heart.

"I'm not sure—"

"Look at this place, it's perfect. It's peaceful."

I do. The gentle lapping of the aquamarine water and the delicate white sand, the sheer drop of the limestone cliffs and the green jungle that hugs the rocks like they were its children. My heart throbs.

"Maybe we should wait?" I try to swallow, but my mouth is dry, and my eyes feel heavy with tears.

"For what?"

I shake my head, caught off guard. We said we would set her free, let her ashes fly in the wind and be scattered, allow her spirit to roam wild and free; but I don't think I was prepared for the moment to arrive. Maya didn't prepare me, I'm not ready to let go.

"Let's go." She starts walking towards a trail hidden within the dense shrubbery, but my legs won't budge, and I can't move.

When I don't follow, Maya turns back around, she slithers her hand through mine and takes a step forcing my feet forward.

"I'm not ready," my voice cracks.

"Neither am I," she admits as she guides us into the cool canopy of the trail.

We make the journey in a heavy silence, my sweaty hand laced in my sister's as we ascend the hill. I don't even know where it leads; all I know is that, at the end of this journey, I'll have to say goodbye. Again. And even though it's been final for a while, this feels even more so—heavier, harder. My legs wobble as we near the top and Maya holds me up, a towering pillar of strength. She's always been stronger than me, better than me.

We emerge into the bright sunlight; it stings my skin after the coolness of the canopy, and I blink a few times, my eyes adjusting to the brightness. When they do, I draw in a sharp breath.

The island lies beneath us. The expanse of the crystalline ocean as far as the eyes can see as we tower above the beach where the other guests look like swarming, uninvited insects. Maya was right. This place is perfect.

We stand for a while, time an uncharted thing; just the light breeze and the sun and the lazy waves and my sister's hand in mine.

Her movement jerks me out of my lull. Maya sets her bag down and bends after it, digging inside. Under different circumstances, I would have made a joke about the kitchen sink; but as she pulls out our mother's urn, a thick lump lodges in my throat.

"Are you ready?" *I'll never be ready.*

I do something with my head that she translates as a nod and starts to unscrew the urn.

The lump scratches all the way down my throat as I swallow it like a bitter serrated pill. I stare at the urn. It holds the last remnants of the woman who carried me, raised me, and showed me what love is.

Maya grips the urn, white bleeding into her knuckles, the light breeze fluttering her few loose strands of hair. We lock eyes in a silent agreement, but not the same one. We've never been good at communicating, and we've always gone in opposite directions, which is why we should have seen this coming.

I step forward to reach for the urn so that we could release our mother together, but at the very moment, Maya lets loose her remains. As if in a dream, I knock the half empty urn from her hands.

I watch, suspended in horrified fascination, as it plummets and explodes on the limestone ground, splattering the vegetation and our feet in splashes of grey and pasty white. As if on cue, the wind drops, and the air stands as still as my mother's heart.

"What did you do?" Maya screams at me looking horror stricken at the grey patch now covering the green grass at our feet.

"I didn't… I wasn't… it's not…" I stammer, but nothing seems to come out as I look at the carnage around us. I shake my head frantically like a bobblehead on a dashboard.

"This wasn't meant to be like this. You ruin everything Abi!"

"What?" My head whiplashes, and I stare at my sister. "How is this my fault? I didn't make the wind stop."

"*You* ruined it." Her eyes swell with tears and her body begins to tremble, "You're so irresponsible and selfish."

"What?" I take a step back as her eyes narrow and her tear-stricken face turns a bright shade of red.

"You always do what *you* want, flaunting your responsibilities, go gallivanting in the nights, take off to see the world."

"Maya…"

"You're so wild, so free, so fucking careless."

"That's not fair, I—"

"You're. Just. Like. Her!" she screams at me and her chin falls on her chest.

She sniffles then falls to her knees, reaching into her bag and pulling out a small pack of tissues. Her motherhood engraved into her being. She blows long and hard and tucks the tissue into the pocket of her sundress. "You're just like her," she repeats, and her tears come hard and fast. Her chest rises and falls as she pulls in long harsh breaths, "And I can't stand it."

"Maya?" I take a tentative step towards her, but she crawls over to the mess and starts collecting the shattered pieces of our mother's urn.

"She loved you most because you were just like her, you guys could always connect on a level me and her never could. She gave you her wild spirit and left me to shoulder all the responsibilities."

"You know she loved you," I say soothingly as I bend and start to collect shattered pieces. I try not to think of the course grey particles that tint the pads of my fingers. "And you were always so strong, so capable..."

"It didn't mean I needed her any less. I *had* to be strong, cause *you* had her undivided attention."

"That's not fair." I stand up cupping the ceramic pieces in my hand, "You've always known what you wanted to be, and where you wanted to end up in life, and you did. You have an amazing career and two beautiful kids, a happy marriage—you got everything you wanted."

She scoffs, "Everything I wanted? I wanted a piece of her, as strong and heavily engraved as yours."

I sigh and set the pieces down, then reach for my sister's chin. I coax it up until she looks at me, "Maya, don't you see? You got the best pieces of her." She shakes her head, and I force her gaze back to mine, "She taught you how to love, intensely and without doubt. You are the best mom in the world to those kids. You're fiercely protective of me, even when I don't want you to be. You are strong, loyal and kind, but most of all, she gave you her smile." My heart pangs as I search my sister's face, seeing my mom etched in her features "Her gentle eyes and her dark hair. You get to see her every day when you look into the mirror, you get a reminder of how much of her you actually have."

Maya's hands collapse at her side and the pile of ceramic pieces drop from her hands and clatter beneath us as she throws herself at me and sobs into my neck.

"Me too," I say as I tighten my grip around my sister. I let her cry as I hold her. For as long as she needs it. it's the first time I feel like she's ever needed me.

When her sobs subside, I open my mouth again. "This is just so typical of her," I say and Maya pulls away her, lips a thin tight line, she dips her chin once. "Remember that time she planned my fourteenth birthday party? She invited everyone even though I asked her not to, and everyone showed up a day early cause she got the date wrong?"

"You spent that evening crying your heart out."

I nod, the memory hooking through my heart and tugging. "And you know her, she brushed it off and said, 'mistakes are inevitable, they remind us that we're still not perfect.'"

We say the last in unison. My mother having repeated the sentiment hundreds of times over our lifetime, and both our mouths curve up in tight, fragile smiles.

We wrap our arms around one another again, and her embrace is warm and kind and drenched in sorrow. We break apart and stare at the grey spatter coating the grass.

"Ready?" She asks, taking the reins again.

I nod. We turn away and step towards the path when a gust of wind picks. We whirl back to see it pick up some of the ash and carry it over the ocean.

"Bye, eema," I whisper, and we make our way back down the trail. The way down somehow lighter but still burdened. My emotions flying in every direction, unsettled like a blustering wind inside me.

A beautiful numbness falls on me as we spend the rest of the day in the sun. I'm aware of eating and getting back onto the boat and sitting in a bus and getting back to our room, but it all feels like it's happening to someone else. I can't shake the feeling of losing her all over again.

Chapter Fourteen

Abi

Maya wants to go for dinner, but I shake my head climbing into my bed and covering myself with a sheet. She bends over me and places a delicate and unexpected kiss on my cheek then leaves the room. The empty silence is overbearing. I can hear my sadness, it booms in my ears, or maybe that's the sound of my heart breaking all over again.

My phone dings and a message flashes across the screen. As much as I want to ignore it, I picture Maya at some take away joint waiting for my reply. If I pretend, I didn't see the message, I'll just get an earful when she gets back. I sigh and reach for my phone, but when I look at the screen, it's not what I expect.

'Can I interest you in some rum?'

I smile at his joke and stare at the phone for a while. The heaviness keeps pulling me back down. After a long while I text back.

'Not tonight'

The screen flashes right away and the phone starts to ring in my hands.

"Can't handle rejection?" I say in a quiet voice.

"I might be a little hurt, but I'm a big boy."

I sigh and wonder if he's smirking. On any other day, I would have stroked his ego just as enthusiastically as I would his cock, but tonight I need a beat. When I don't answer for a while, his voice changes.

"Hey, did I...?"

"No, no," my voice rises a few notches and my heart somersaults in my chest, I can't handle two losses in one week. "It's just... we let her ashes go today."

"What's your room number?" His voice changes, tinted with notes of urgency.

"You can't—"

"Room number?"

"Maya—"

"What's the number pirate?"

"Sixteen," I whisper into the phone. A second later the line goes dead on the other end.

I lay awake, my mind swirls with thoughts and my body coils and churns with anticipation. An hour later, when Maya's come back and Seth hasn't shown up, it's replaced by a heavy disappointment doused with more guilt. I hate that I keep feeling this way.

I toss and turn, listening to Maya's soft snores fill the room. Her words echo in my head.

She loved you most cause you're just like her.

You're. Just. Like. Her.

Time turns into a deep black hole that sucks me inside. In the emptiness, I'm forced to examine the last twenty-eight years of my life. Every stupid mistake and failed relationship, every impulsive decision, and the aftermath.

My life is a mess.

I'm nothing like her.

I'm drowning in my past, examining old wounds, and comparing myself to my mom when I hear a soft rapping. I strain my ears and listen. I hear it a second time. My eyes jerk over to Maya's still form before I hop out of the bed and go to the door.

I crack it open and find Seth standing on the other side. My mouth drops open a little and my stomach flips when I see his stern expression. His sharp jaw tightened and bunched up.

"What are you doing here?" I whisper as my heart swells.

He remains silent and tries to step into the room. I block him with my body holding onto the edge of the door. "You can't—" I whisper yell at him.

He doesn't let me finish. Instead, he pushes the door open, lets himself in, and sweeps me into his arms in one swift movement. He feels so fucking good. His warmth soaks into me, permeating my skin, flowing inside me, till some of the sadness lifts and I can somehow breathe again. When I draw in breath, I breathe him in—his scent. He smells like sunshine and salt and Seth, and I lick my lips. I don't mean to. His arms tighten around me and my tears threaten to spill again, and my body rages with raw, strange emotions. I cling onto him, needing his strength.

A low moan drifts from my sister's bed as she flaps around. I snap myself away from him and push against his chest. His eyes follow the sound to Maya's bed. My shoulders sink. I bring a finger to my lips then point to the door.

He can't be here. I need time. My heart needs time.

He nods. He understands. My lower lip wobbles. I already miss his warmth.

When he starts to move, it's not towards the door but to my bed. I freeze. My heart stutters. He kicks off his shoes and stretches along the length of my bed. His soft eyes lock onto mine.

I shake my head again and point to the door. He shrugs,

feigning misunderstanding. I roll my eyes despite myself. I edge closer to my bed, point at him stiffly, then point at the door, my lips move with silent words. He ignores me, tapping the empty space by his side.

I take another step towards the bed and point at him. In a blur of movement he bolts up, grabs my wrist, and pulls me onto the bed beside him. His hand slithers over my mouth, muffling the yelp that escapes my lips. We lay motionless. Waiting. My wide eyes bounce around the room as I listen to my thundering heart and hold my breath. When there's nothing but silence, his hand slips from my mouth and he glues me against him; my back to his chest, his arms closing like steel bands around me.

"Shhh," he whispers in my ear, "just let me hold you." His voice vibrates against my skin and he places a single kiss on my shoulder. We're still as he holds me, his hot breath skimming over my skin, his smell engulfs me like his strong arms.

I'm too tired to fight, my mind is too exhausted to think about how I'll explain it all to Maya. And the truth is, his arms around me make me feel good. Safe. Like I could heal. He buries his head in my neck, and I push myself tighter against him.

We lie in silence, only my mind screaming and my heart cracking as if it's made of fragile bones. My body shakes with soundless tears, my eyes burn. He feels like a furnace on a cold winter's day, I just want to curl up against him and sleep my worries away. So I let my eyes close.

When I wake up, my bed is empty, but somehow, I feel whole.

∞

את

∞

Seth

I peel my sweaty shirt from my body, thankful for the air con in my hotel room. The short ride on the bike back to my hotel reminded me how tired I am.

I can't help the smile that creeps along my face when I slide my fingers across the screen to accept her call, "Good morning pirate."

"You weren't here when I woke up." She's talking in a hushed tone, and I can only assume she's hiding from her sister.

"Seemed like it might get us both into trouble." I hear her soft chuckle and revel in the sound. I prefer her happy.

"Thank you." There is so much weight behind those two words, I can feel the emotion through the earpiece.

"No worries Abi," my eyes burn with exhaustion and I can still smell her on my skin. She was so soft and so vulnerable last night, I could have taken her a hundred different ways. But that's not what she needed, and I am overwhelmed with the desire to give her what she needs. I want to take care of her, I want to make her mine.

"Bounty hunter?" she whispers

"Yeah?"

"What's your room number?"

I chuckle into the phone and can't help the way my stomach tightens with anticipation. "Twenty-three."

The line goes dead. I chuck it on the bedstand while collapsing onto the bed and falling asleep with a stupid grin on my face.

Chapter Fifteen

Abi

Maya was right to scatter the ashes when we did. It was like raising an anchor that's been weighing us down. We came up to the surface and were suddenly able to gulp long drags of air. It was a long and sticky band aid that was ripped off an open wound. It still stung, still hurt, still felt deep and raw—and yet, it allowed healing to begin.

I spend the next four days soaking up the sun and drenching myself in memories of my mother. We allow ourselves to laugh and cry at her expense. We let ourselves be free without words and emotions, and we eat and drink and douse ourselves in sunshine and salty water.

We buy handmade bracelets and cheap imitation brand name shirts. I read two whole books while digging my feet into the sand. And then there were the nights when Maya would finally go to sleep, and I'd sneak out of my bed and fall into Seth's. Wrapped up in his arms and his sheets, we spent the darkest hours talking and laughing and exploring each other in naked, sweaty bliss. I never wanted it to end. The notion of being away from him gnawed at me.

It's been so easy to get swept away by Seth. He's a calm to the storm that crashed through my life, setting aside the wreckage, and putting things back together. I didn't want to think about the part when his calm was gone and all that would be left is reality.

Chapter Sixteen

Abi

"It's our last night, I thought we could hang out." Maya is in her pajamas, looking relaxed with her wet hair and sun kissed skin. She slips under her bedcovers and pats the empty space next to her. "Movie night?"

I bite the inside of my cheek and look down at my phone. It's well after eight and I know where I want to spend my last night in Thailand, and it's definitely not watching chick flicks in my sister's bed. I think about the last week, how hard she's tried to patch up years of anger between us. She's pushing the proverbial olive branch in my face, and even though my stomach drops and my heart pinches and my skin burns, I conjure up my best smile as I step towards her bed. "Sure."

She claps her hands a few times then grabs the remote, she's already ordered the film and if I know my sister, she's probably ordered two more to follow. I slip into the bed next to her and she rests her head on my shoulder. "This is going to be so much fun."

I nod, and the knot in my stomach turns into a swarm of

restlessness. *Not the kind of fun I was hoping to have.* Guilt rams through my stomach and the swarm wakes, stinging my insides.

Maya watches the movie while I watch the clock. I'm pretty sure it's broken. It's like the minutes don't want to move and the movie goes on forever. Maya giggles and awes and oohs, I want to make those sounds too. *But not here.* I bite down the thought and wait; my skin feels like it's shrinking the longer I sit and wait, I just want to burst.

It's after midnight when Maya's head finally drops onto the pillow and her light shallow snores put me out of my misery.

I have five hours left with Seth if I can find a fast enough taxi to get me to his hotel room.

The hot wind lashes across my face as I hold onto the motorcycle taxi driver. He swerves and swoops around the endless traffic and drunken revelers that seem to spill from the sidewalk and flood the road. This place feels alive, it has its own pounding heartbeat that never stops or slows, and I revel in the chaos of it.

I swing off the bike, pay the driver, and run up to Seth's room—my body charged with surging emotion as I see darkness under his door.

I knock quietly and hold my breath. My heart thrashes wildly in my chest.

Five seconds pass, then ten. Then an eternity. My heart drops and dread tries to crawl over me, but before it slithers around my neck, the lock clicks and the door swings open.

Seth stands on the other side, ruffled hair, naked torso, and charming smile. He looks delicious and the tip of my tongue slips out to lick my lips. He's holding something in his hand.

"I thought you weren't coming." The way he says it makes it sound like he isn't talking about me being here. My heart seizes until my lungs beg for air. A smirk stretches across his beautiful face.

"I was delayed."

"Your ship broke down again?"

I nod, biting down a smile, "I had to deal with my head of engineering."

"And how did that go?"

"Let's just say, I'm not planning on being here in the morning." My joke falls flat as the impact of my words jolts us.

Seth recovers first and opens the door wider for me. I step inside, my gaze traveling to his hand. "What's that?"

"Why, it's your shot of rum, Pirate."

"Oh, bounty hunter," I step in closer and graze my lips along his, he sucks in a sharp breath that makes me burn for him. "When will you learn? I'm just a humble smuggler, and not the bounty you so desperately seek."

He grips my hip with his free hand and pulls me to him, "That's okay, I'd much rather spend my night plundering your treasures."

"Oh," I groan and roll my eyes as his mouth curls up into a grin. Before I can say anything about the cheese factor of his comeback, his mouth covers mine in a hot, hungry kiss that has him slamming the door with my back pinned to it. He keeps kissing me, long and hard and deep, and I wonder if he's trying to use his tongue to erase his last statement. I don't even care.

He breaks the kiss and steps away, setting the unspilled shot glass on the table. I glance over and see that it's set up with two place settings and some fresh flowers. His face colours a little as he notices me noticing.

"I thought—"

"—I'm sorry."

We start at the same time, but the words die mid-sentence. There's no point lamenting lost time but enjoy whatever time we have left with one another. It's as if the thought crashes into us at the same time, and we rip at the space between us, launching ourselves at each other.

Sound is torn from the room and all that's left is the thundering of my heart as his lips crash against mine in a possessive, urgent kiss. One hand sinks into my hair as he draws me closer, still deepening the kiss, demanding more, while the other winds around me like a chain. He steps forwards, backing me up till my knees hit the bed.

∞

אותו

∞

I like the way he's looking at me, his tousled hair in a frantic mess and his brow beaded with sweat. He leans on an elbow as his long fingers draw lazy circles around my belly button and stroke up to just between my breasts. It's delicious and taunting and sweet, and my stomach knots with anxiety.

"I'm going to miss you," I whisper.

Part of me wishes he doesn't hear, and the other part screams for him to say the same. It's only been a week. A stressful one for both of us, one that propelled us into crazy emotions and crazier notions. We've spent every spare minute we had in each other's arms—laughing, loving, connecting—and I can't believe that it's just skin deep. I can't believe that all I'll ever get of Seth is this one week.

"Me too." He kisses my shoulder and relief spreads inside me like warm chocolate sauce.

"Yeah?"

"Well, maybe a little bit." He teases and finds my lips. He kisses me slowly, decadently, like I'm a dessert he wants to saver. The feeling of him makes my whole body ignite.

He wrenches away, pulls himself from the bed and winks at me before going to the bathroom. I sink into the mattress, staring at the ceiling fan that roars lazily above my head. It feels like a ticking clock, like it's mocking me, reminding me that we're running out of time. Jitters crawl along my skin as uncertainty grips me. I want to ask him if he wants more, I want to know if I could be more for him; but then, he did just leave another relationship and tell me I was clingy. Even if he was joking, I have to wonder how much merit lies behind his words. Maybe he needs space. An ocean of space.

I cover my face, my palms circling my eyes as I try to pry the answers from my tired, aching brain. When nothing happens, I grab the sheet, wrap it around me and make my way to the window.

His reflection appears in the dark pane. Neon lights from the bar across the road paint his flesh in greens and pinks and highlight his bronzed, muscular arms. A white towel clings to his hips and I feel the weight of his gaze on me.

"So," he says and pushes a hand through his wet hair, tousling the strands.

"So," I respond.

Neither of us move, our eyes remain locked through the window. Like we're looking at alternate versions of ourselves, ones that could afford to do so much more. Be so much more.

He takes a single step closer, "What now?"

"Now?"

"Tomorrow. The day after that. Us, me? You?" He blurts it out, his hands stabbing the air.

"Us? Tomorrow?" I furrow an eyebrow as a smoldering ember ignites inside of me. I want to cling to his words as tightly as I cling to my sheet. "Tomorrow I go back to being a smuggler and you go back to chasing your bounties."

"What if I want to chase you instead?"

His words shiver through me and my heartstrings quiver. I close my eyes, wondering how life could be with Seth, how we could make this work. If we could. I take a deep breath, putting out the fires of doubt sparking to life inside me and filling myself with hope. "I'll be hard to catch."

He nods, "You can let me try."

"I want you to." And I do, oh so much. My heart falters in my chest. But still, I can't allow all this happiness to flood the room. Not just yet. Not till it's real, not till it drips through every part of me.

Seth takes another step towards me, the jest fallen from his face. "Do you want to try Abi? Do you want me to catch you?"

My blood courses hot under my skin as I take in his face, my eyes drop to his lips, his smooth mouth, and the rugged scruff on his jaw. I have a sudden urge to run my hands across his whiskers and wrap myself around him, bury my head in his neck and inhale him. But I don't, instead I tear my eyes away and stare into the bleak night. Flashing neon lights, and drunken tourists slash by the window. I feel Seth's eyes boring into me, sense his approach, every inch of my skin alert and then he's there. His chest drumming my back in a haphazard rhythm that seers my back, his breaths in my ear, harsh and sharp, sending shivers down my body in torrid waves.

His fingers creep along my nape, trace my collar bone then grasp the strands of my messy hair. He brushes them away from my shoulder and lays a delicate kiss on my neck, my body erupts in goosebumps. He tugs at my hair, exposing my neck. My body riots as his rough fingers draw a slow line from my neck trailing the length of my arm till our fingers touch and lace. His hands are rough and soft and fit perfectly with mine.

"Long distance hardly ever works," I whisper wanting the darkness to swallow my doubts.

"We can try to make it work…" his breath feathers my skin, "I want to try, with you."

A tear slides down my flushed cheek and I nod, unable to speak. My eyes slam shut and my breath quivers as I allow myself to lean against him, draw on his warmth, his strength.

His hand wraps around my body, settling across my stomach and cementing us together. I want to sink, to melt, to disappear into Seth.

"I want to try with you too." I shed my doubts and fears and let the sheet slip out of my grip. Seth untangles his hand from the fabric and lets it pool at our feet, his eyes roam my reflection, his teeth dig into his lower lip. He takes in my flushed face, my dark eyes, my parted lips. Stealing down to my breasts my nipples pebble at the cold air or maybe at the intensity of his stare. I want him to touch me. But his eyes keep sliding down to my stomach, to my pussy. I squirm under his gaze. Even the glass can't protect me from its fervor.

"Seth," I moan at him, squeezing my thighs together. The hard ridge of his cock throbs against my back. He looks up then. When our eyes clash, his glint with hungry desire, his jaw tightens, and body hardens.

He grips my chin and forces my face to his before taking my lips. He kisses me so greedily I whimper, but it's lost in his mouth. My hand slides to the back of his neck, drawing him to me. I need him… so much more of him. I need his heat and his tongue and his hands, and it's like he knows. He deepens the kiss, sending a tremor of want and need through me.

Seth feels good, his heat pushes away the coldness inside me. But I need even more, I want to burn. I kiss him hungrily wanting the fire inside him to spill into me. I slide my free hand onto his, slowly guiding him between my legs.

"Fuck," he grinds out husky and low. His fingers touch my wetness and his other hand falls from my jaw and pinches a nipple. I whimper into his possessive mouth, the one that owns me.

His hands work my body while his mouth drags away from mine and lays kisses along my neck and shoulder. All I can do is fall against him and let him chase the darkness away.

My hands feel empty, the snatched touches I manage to steal aren't enough. I reach behind me and find his erection, he's so hard. His thick cock twitches in my hands and he lets out a hoarse groan. His hands drop from my body and jerk my hands away. "No!" He growls then drives me against the cold window, forcing my face back to his, kissing me hard and deep. The coolness spreads on my cheek, into my neck down my slick body.

His grip retains me against the pane while his mouth nibbles and bites and kisses the length of my bare back to my ass and back again, sucking and grazing my skin, sparking all the nerves in my body.

"Seth," I whimper as his powerful body looms over mine, caging me against the glass. And then he thrusts inside me, stealing my breath. He thrusts a second time before I find his decadent mouth, and his kiss makes my head swim.

His hand hooks around me and finds its way back down to my wetness. I arch into him, everything on fire. My palms sprawl on the glass, my head whips back. I meet the savage pounding of his hips, hungry for my release, and his fingers tease and swirl till I moan out his name. He slams into me till my entire body comes apart and pleasure explodes across my body. His hands lock around me and he pulls me into him, harder, deeper as my pussy clenches around him. His body jerks in a broken rhythm.

"Fuck," he grunts. His teeth sink into my shoulder, fingers dig into my flesh, his slick body glued to mine, his heaving chest rising and falling while I try to find air to fill my lungs. "Fuck," he pants over a wrecked breath, his heavy body rests over me.

When he regains himself, he lifts me up and takes us both back to the bed. He kisses me. It's one of his sweet kisses. One of those kisses that are honey mixed with lemon—potent in its urgency, in its possessiveness, yet lavish and deep and all the shades of sunshine.

Seth is happiness.

We don't talk much more, just feel each other. I can't imagine not having my hands on him tomorrow. Even as I think it, my alarm blares and screams, and suddenly it feels like I've taken a breath and sunk under water. Sound is muted below the rippling current, my lungs burn and my heart hammers and all I have to do is break the surface.

Leaving Seth feels like drowning.

He doesn't release me. And I don't want him to. I want to drown in him instead. His bruised lips latch onto my body, his teeth graze my nipples, my skin, my lips. His fingers dig into my hips, his tongue lashes and swirls. He's leaving me marked—like I belong to him and he wants his scent all over me to ensure other males keep their distance. I love that I am covered by his scent. My inner thighs still coated with him after he pulled out, like a souvenir I get to take home from my holiday. Until I shower that is. Showering suddenly sounds like the worst idea ever.

The alarm blares again, and this time we wrench ourselves away. I feel the disconnect. It hurts. It's like being cut open. We are cleaved apart.

We dress. The silence between us suddenly heavy, forlorn.

What if we can't make it work?

I grab my bag and take a final quick look around the

room. When I've run out of reasons and excuses to prolong the inevitable, I break our silence. "I'll call you when I land," I say unsure what else there is to say that would not end up in me stripping back down and missing my flight.

"I might still be in the air," he shrugs, "but I'll call back."

I nod. *Are we already failing at this?*

Seth grips my wrist and pulls me to him. Our eyes clash and his lips brush over mine, ever so lightly, setting a small fire deep in my belly.

"We will make it work; Israel isn't that far away," he says it with such certainty, so much confidence, that it strengthens my insides. I believe him. I want to so badly. He draws me into him and we kiss. It's long and deep and decadent and it doesn't feel like goodbye, even when it should.

He smacks my ass and pushes away from me. "Get out of here now or I won't not be able to let you go smuggler."

I smirk, step over to the table and grab the shot of rum. I tip it back, allowing the drink to blaze down my throat.

"See you soon, bounty hunter." I wink and rush to the door before either of us realizes what a stupid mistake we're making.

As I slam the door behind me, I hear him call out, "I knew it!"

∞

הדבר

∞

My heart throbs. It feels strained and tired, like it's been working too hard. The erratic beats like an unconventional song whose rhythm slows or speeds up at a whim.

Everywhere I look I see Seth.

The hotel bed I never slept in, the terminal bustling with people, boarding my flight and sitting next to an empty seat that in seconds would be taken by my sister. The only thing I have left to hold onto as we take off is his smell still embedded into my skin.

The engine whines and the plane moves around the tarmac. Maya grabs my hand as we take off, and I can't help but wonder if I've just made the biggest mistake of my life.

Chapter Seventeen

Abi

I wake up with a muffled groan and pull the blanket over my head. I can't be awake already. I feel like I've barely slept. The body forgets so easily how hard it is to fly in and out of different time zones and maintain some kind of normal rhythm. My body is out of sync, everything is out of sync. Mostly Seth and me.

I grab the phone and find another missed message from him and my heart pangs. I check my clock. If I call him now it would be 3 a.m.

I miss the sound of his voice. I miss his low, husky laughter that rumbled over me and swept me away. It's already been six weeks without him, and the feelings haven't subsided. In fact, they've intensified. I sigh and slide my finger over my phone unlocking it and read over Seth's message.

7th Sept 20.07
Hey, did you dream about me? Was it good? Is that why you're smiling?

My lips curl into a smile as I picture him typing the message.

8th Sept 08.05
No. I actually dreamt about another bounty hunter.

I set my phone down, a self-satisfied grin on my face and get ready for the day.

8th Sept 23.23
Yeah? Me too.

9th Sept 00.12
Was he as hot and sexy as the one I dreamt about?

9th Sept 04.11
Hotter and sexier.

9th Sept 3.17
Sounds delicious, can I meet him?

10th Sept 05.23
I've already killed him

10th Sept 10.55
Your dream boy?

10th Sept 11.36
If you're thinking about him instead of me, he has to go.

I giggle at his possessiveness and liquid heat flows through my veins.

11th Sept 06.07
I thought you're meant to capture them alive.

11th Sept 07.15
Semantics. I miss you.

12th Sept 8.19

I miss you too. Like crazy. I wish you were here.

12th Sept 23.58
Me too. But we'll do that video chat you've been promising
me. I can't wait to see you.

13th Sept 8.43

Ditto

Chapter Eighteen

Seth

The phone flashes with Abi's number and I suddenly feel like a complete blundering idiot dropping the phone and feeling sweat form across my forehead. I've missed her so much since Thailand and our stunted text messages just haven't felt the same. Between the time differences and her job, I worry that she was right, that maybe we can't make it work; but as her face appears on the screen, all my fears are alleviated, replaced by intense laughter.

Abi stands in a bedroom. She's wearing a black, pirate captain hat and an eye patch. Her long hair is braided into two long plaits that fall on either side of her face and she's biting down on her red-hot fucking lips.

I catch myself and suck in a breath settling down the laughter, but unable to hold back my stupid grin. "Pirate," I greet her and my whole body feels how much I miss her.

"Bounty hunter," she replies, not missing a beat. Her lips curl into a mischievous smile that I want pressed against mine. Fuck I want to taste her again.

"You've been hard to catch."

"Maybe you're just not very good at your job." She winks at me and my body throbs with need.

We spend some time catching up. She tells me about her job and other mundane shit while I talk to her about my life. The one that doesn't include her in it every single day. My heart stammers and I wish we were having this conversation in our house—one we share. I could hold her hand while she talks, my thumb would draw circles on the back of her hand, and her eyes would be creased by laughter lines, and I'd be able to kiss her any time I wanted. Steal her words and her breath away and make every part of her mine.

"Seth?"

I hear my name through the fog of my thoughts, and I find her beautiful eyes staring at me through the small cold screen.

"Where did you go?"

"Sorry, I was just thinking."

"Did you hurt yourself?" she smirks, and I scoff.

"Only a little."

"What were you thinking about?"

"About how much I miss you and want you."

"Oh?" She puts the phone down and steps backward so that slowly, she reveals the rest of her outfit. "And if you had me, what would you do with me?"

My mouth falls open and I'm somewhere between admiration, shock and fucking awe.

She is wearing a leather corset, the laces in the front slightly loose to reveal just enough of her breasts to make my mouth water. The black number hugs her torso and ends in a lacy hem that covers just a little of her naked thighs, where a holster is strapped on the left is holstering what looks like a plastic pistol.

She's stunning and sexy and hilarious, and I love that she's gone to this length to play our game. I'm totally unmatched, but right now as my cock strains against my jeans, I don't give any fucks. I just hate that she's so far away and I can't touch her.

She bites down on her lips and color floods her cheeks when the silence between us stretches.

"Fuck Abi, you look…" I swallow, my mouth suddenly a desert, my body tightens. Her teeth sink deeper into her lower lip and all I want is to kiss her. I want them wrapped around my cock again. I clear my throat, "I'd undo those laces… so I can bind your hands together and make sure you don't escape."

"Awe Bounty hunter, if you did that, I wouldn't be able to do this."

I'm riveted. My eyes glued to the screen when her hand reaches over to the laces and she pulls ever so slowly. They unthread agonizingly slow and as the corset opens up a little more, I can see a hint of her dusky nipples.

My hands grip the edge of my seat and clench around the hard wood as I remember what she felt like in my arms. My cock strains in my jeans and I let out a stuttered breath, "I'd peel that underwear off you."

I watch as she lifts the lacy hem of the corset and sticks her thumbs into the elastic of the black lingerie she wears beneath. Then once again, as if she's on slow motion, she peels them away allowing the hem to fall over and cover that junction between her thighs—where I wish my mouth could explore and fingers could feel and cock could sink. I'm so hard it hurts. I undo the button of my jeans and let my hand roll over my swollen cock.

"I want to touch you," I say in a husky breathy voice I hardly recognize as my own.

"Where?" She sounds shy, trying to be bold, and it's so fucking sexy I think I'll explode in my pants.

"Everywhere," I breathe out.

I don't know what to expect. I'm mesmerized, spell bound and so fucking hard.

She grabs her phone again and resets it, then stalks onto the bed on her knees. Her legs folded behind her, her thighs open wide, her back slightly arched. I can see all of her and still she's covered. I grit my teeth in agony.

Her hand curls around one of the edges of the open corset and runs up and down deliberately slow. She moans a little each time her fingers brush over her nipple. My hands hurt from grabbing the chair so tightly, and I don't know exactly when I leaned so close to the screen. I push back on the chair wanting to scream at her. I want her to throw that fucking thing open and show me her body, I want to kiss her skin and bite her nipples, fuck her like an animal till she calls out my name. Instead, I sit and suffer as she tortures me with her teasing movements and low moans.

Her other hand slips between her legs obscured by the lace. I can see it moving, but it's not clear, not focused, and it's driving me completely insane.

"Like this Bounty Hunter?" Her breathy sultry voice shoots straight to my cock as it jolts in my boxers, begging to be touched. A spot of pre cum stains the fabric.

I swallow hard, "I want to see more."

She stops moving and runs her tongue over her top lip, "That will cost you."

I'm ready to sell my house, my soul, and every other precious possession just to get a glimpse of Abi touching her body. "What do you want?" I barely manage.

"Mm mm, how about you show me yours and I'll show you mine?" Her lips curl into a sly grin.

"One sec." I say as I pull down my jeans and boxers. This is the easiest price I've ever had to pay. I hold my aching cock in my hand and tip the phone down, "h\Happy?" I ask and flash it back to my face.

"Not as happy as you," she grins, then narrows her eyes, "but I want to see more."

"Typical." I grunt.

She just nods and teases me a little, nudging the corset open just a fraction more, reminding me what's at stake. The painful swelling in my cock is enough reminder, but the slight movement spurs me into action. I set the phone down in such a way that she can see my face, torso and cock. "satisfied?" I grunt out.

"About to be."

I choke out a broken chuckle as Abi rips open the corset and I get to see her perfect fucking tits; her nipples are so hard and tight and my mouth waters at the thought of them. I fiddle around a drawer and find some hand lotion. It's not ideal, but watching Abi taking complete possession of her own body, exploring it in front of me—for me—while dressed like the sluttiest pirate on Earth, is sending jolts of electricity through my bones and I can't take it anymore. I grab my cock and start stroking as Abi's hand slips downward. She pulls the lacy hem up and reveals her pink, wet pussy, and all I want to do is jump into the screen and devour her.

Abi moans as her fingers circle her clit, and I grind my jaw through my growing pleasure. My hand tightens around my shaft. I'm vaguely aware of her eyes on me, but I can't hold back anymore. Pumping harder and faster till the familiar tightening grips my lower belly and travels along my lower back. My balls tighten and I head rears back, jaw clenched. The numbness creeps into my body and eats away at my mind. A beautiful, delicious fog that makes the world almost vanish in its entirety and all that exists is an intense, powerful sensation that rushes to a single point of exit.

My eyes screw shut, my spine bows, and I groan as I come all over my stomach like a sixteen-year-old teenager. I sit there, hot come dripping down my abdomen and between my thighs, almost shellshocked as the world comes back into focus. Abi's there. Her body shakes and her moans grow more desperate as she touches herself. My semi-erect cock twitches as I watch completely awestruck the way her hips gyrate to meet the rhythm of her fingers, how her tits bounce with movement, the way her eyes clamp shut, her head falls back, and a raw hungry moan rips from her red pouty lips. She is so fucking beautiful as her orgasm takes control of her body.

She catches her breath. A sweet, shy smile hides behind the teeth that bite down on her lower lip and she collapses onto the bed, hiding herself from me.

"Abi," I say on an unsteady breath and her face breaks into a stunning smile. It hurts that she's so far away, that I can't touch her or feel her warmth or pull her to me and hold her till morning. "Satisfied?"

"Almost." Her smile falters.

"You're very hard to please, aren't you pirate?"

We spend the next hour talking and catching up. She tells me about Maya and her work, and then she peels off the opened corset and gives me another show. I have wanking fodder for months—for eternity—because I'll never get tired of watching her come. And I realise that she's it, and that I would suffer through all my frustration if there was even a slight chance that we could keep making it work.

Chapter Nineteen

3rd Oct 2.17
I miss you

4th Oct 10.43
I miss you more

4th Oct 5.56
This sux

4th Oct 4.15
I know

∞

אתמול

∞

Abi

The clock ticks over and it's midnight. It's November seventeenth and I'm officially twenty-nine and eema isn't here to see it. My heart tightens in my chest as the phone begins to ring.

"Hi baby." His voice is low and careful like he knows how fragile I am. "Happy birthday Abi."

"Thanks," I sniff into the phone.

"I wish—"

"I know." I don't want him to finish because it's bad enough not having eema around. It's my first big milestone without her and it feels insurmountable. A wave of agony washes over me and the tears slide down my face and onto my knees. We sit in silence as he listens to me weep like a baby. When my tears subside, I wipe them away, blow my nose and listen to the static silence on the other end.

"Hello?" My broken voice quivers.

"I'm still here," he says, and I hear the concern in his voice, and his warmth.

"It's late where you are."

"I don't mind. I just want to spend some of your birthday with you, and I wanted to be the first to say it."

"Not much of a celebration." I sniff and fight back more tears.

"Are you saying I don't know how to throw a party?"

I giggle a little as his mock offence and shrug. He can't see me, of course. "Well, your parties are almost as good as your bounty hunting skills."

"Hey!" I hear his smile; it wraps itself around me, and the pain I've been carrying around for the last few days feels a little lighter.

We talk for a while. He fills the silence with his work projects and the fact he's going to be an uncle and how he burned his dinner the night before. And even though it's banal, I want to hear it all, be a part of it, experience it with him.

My chest cramps again.

He yawns for a fifth time.

"You're tired."

"I'll never get tired of you." He says it with so much

conviction. He's so easy to believe. "But yeah, I have a big day tomorrow."

I nod into the dim room forgetting he can't see me.

"Happy birthday, baby," he says again. "Get some sleep for your big day." The line goes dead.

∞

ובטח

∞

There's a loud pounding that reverberates through the room. It sucks me away from my dream. The one where eema sang me happy birthday and Seth gave me a special present. It was warm and cozy and fucking perfect and still the pounding won't go away.

I fall from the bed and shuffle to the door where I'm greeted by a cranky UPS delivery man who's clearly annoyed at my sleep in.

"Abigail Tal?" He sighs impatiently

"Yeah?"

He hands me a box and makes me sign for it before rushing downstairs and getting on with his day.

There is no return address or any details on the white box. I open it slowly. Inside rests a bottle of rum.

A smile creeps across my face and remains there for the rest of the day.

18th Nov 10.37
Thank you for my present

18th Nov 14.56
Did you drink it all?

19th Nov 07.14
Aye aye

But the delicate and ornate bottle which is rimmed by gold, and whose label shows a mythical sea creature wrapping itself around a pirate ship, sits on a shelf where I can look at it and lament and miss Seth. And I know that when the pain gets too much to bear, I could sip on the contents and let the blazing hot liquid remind me of him.

Chapter Twenty

Seth

I'm sick of missing her. Christmas is creeping up, trees and decorations everywhere, annoying carols and mum is already organizing Christmas lunch. I hate the tone of her voice every time she asks me about my plus one. She thinks I've made Abi up to avoid her asking me about my love life. Frustration prickles up my skin and agitation slithers around me. I want Abi with me. I want her here.

I grab my phone and jab at the screen typing out a message, knowing full well she's flying somewhere and won't get it for hours yet. I grind my teeth and suck in a sharp breath, reminding myself that she's worth it.

5th Dec 8.00
Can you get any time off? I want you in my arms.

6th Dec 01.23
I wish I could. I took time off this time last year, and this is our busiest time of year. You really should have met me earlier.

6th Dec 8.09
I really should have.

Years ago. The thought stabs like a serrated knife in my chest.

7th Dec 4.56
We'll see each other again soon.

7th Dec 11.23
Not soon enough.

I toss the phone on the bedside table and punch the mattress hissing out a frustrated grunt. *Not soon enough at all.*

∞

ארצה

∞

Abi

My phone chirps and I take it out of my pocket. Sara, my niece lights the candles with Aba. He holds her much smaller hand in his and guides her from one candle to the next. It's sweet and my heart stammers at the thought of eema. She would have loved this. Missing her comes in waves, but I've learned to ride them. I read Seth's message.

22nd Dec 06.07
Happy Chanukah.

22nd Dec 06.09
Thanks, feels like it's been going on for a week.

22nd Dec 06.12
Ha. Eat another donut for me.

22nd Dec 06.14
I'm starting to feel like one.

22nd Dec 06.17
Well next time I see you, I'll help you work it off.

22nd Dec 06.17
Are you suggesting I'm fat?

22nd Dec 06.22
I wouldn't dare.

22nd Dec 06.23
Good cause I'd hate to stab you.

22nd Dec 06.25
Really? Cause I'd give anything to stab you with my
big fat...

"His what now?" Maya's voice is directly behind me and I
snap the phone away. She's standing over my shoulder and
wiggling her eyebrows at me. Heat burns the tips of my ears
and coats my face and neck.

Guess I'll have to read the rest of his message later. When
I'm alone.

I elbow her and she laughs at me. Aba throws us a suspicious look and Sara runs up to me and wraps her small hands around my thigh. "Why are you laughing Abi?"

I bite down my smile while Maya chips out, "It's cause she's thinking about big, fat doughnuts."

"Why is that funny, eema?"

"Why don't you ask your aunty?" She throws me under the bus, and I pierce her with a look that promises she will pay for it later. She shrugs it off and walks over to the set table where Aba is holding Ran, my nephew, and chatting to Ronnen, her husband. The whole scene looks perfect. Almost.

I open my arms and wait for Sara to jump up at me, I lift her up and give her a big cuddle. "I wasn't laughing cause it's funny, I was laughing because I'm happy."

"That doesn't make any sense."

"Life often doesn't make any sense."

"I don't understand."

"No one does."

"Eema is right about you."

"Oh yeah? What did she say?"

"That you are very strange."

"Does she now?"

"Yeah."

"What else does she say?"

"That you're just like Savta."

I smile and happiness spills inside me like liquid sunshine. I hug my niece and make our way to the table, feeling eema right there with us.

∞

לנשק

∞

Seth

Sweat trickles down my back and face. I swipe my forehead and wipe my hands on my shorts. The last job is done for the year and I can set the tools down for the next two weeks. A year ago today, I would have gone home to Jess. She would have been dressed and ready, and we would have gone to meet everyone at the foreshore for a few drinks. This year I'll be flying solo.

I pack my ute and lean against the door waiting for Jake to hurry his ass up and get done. I look up at the blue sky and feel its weight on me. Abi is up there somewhere and not here with me, where she belongs. As if she somehow feels my disgruntled mood, my phone chimes with one of her messages.

23rd Dec 0.5.07
I just got an email saying there's a package waiting for me at home. What did you do?

A smile creeps on my face as I think about the gift I sent her.

23rd Dec 05.09
It's your Christmas gift.

23rd Dec 05.12
You got me a Christmas present?

23rd Dec 05.13
It's the done thing.

23rd Dec 05.16

Oh. Thanks. I'm sorry I didn't get you anything.

23rd Dec 05.17
Typical pirate.

23rd Dec 05.19
Hey! I'm a smuggler. And now you've made me feel bad.

I picture her frown. The way her eyebrows dig in and her lip pouts all crinkled at the edges. Its sexy as fuck and my body hardens just thinking about those full sexy lips of hers.

23rd Dec 05.22
The only thing I want is you.

She doesn't answer for a long time and I can't blame her. I don't want to make her feel guilty, but I'm growing restless without her. This relationship is starting to feel like a seesaw; on the days I get to speak to her, to see her face, to watch her exquisite body do incredible things, I'm so high that I cling to that happiness, to her vision, to the sound of her voice, to the knowing that she belongs to me and she will be in my arms soon.

But then there are other days. Days like the last few where the messages are stinted, and our time is almost nonexistent, and I feel her absence gnawing on me. Then I plummet. I battle the feelings of all-consuming agitation and frustration. I'm forced to shove them away, keeping myself busy throughout the day. I push my body harder and farther than I should, all to keep my mind away from her and firmly in whatever it is that occupies me.

I shove the phone back in my pocket just as Jake walks up and throws his tools in the back, making his way to the passenger side. "You ready for a drink?"

"Fuck yeah," I say. Maybe I can drown away my growing impatience.

I keep checking my phone. But it remains silent till my head hits the pillow in a room that should be spinning less.

Her text comes too early in the morning and my head is still swimming when I read it.

24th Dec 06.26
I'll make it up to you.

I smile and put the phone down. *Yes, she will.*

∞

אותך

∞

Were sitting in the lounge, Jake and dad are at it again, politics and the future. I switch off and stare at the tree. Something about those little flickering lights is hypnotizing. I'm full of food and beer. As always, the house is loud and rowdy, mum is laughing with Laura, Lachie's wife, and Mel, Jake's new girlfriend—that mum has tried to position on the outside of all the family photos… Just in case.

My phone pings in short succession and I pull it from my pocket.

25th Dec 18.07
OMG I can't believe it thank you.

25th Dec 18.07
It's amazing I love it.

25th Dec 18.07
Merry Christmas. Thank you.

I grin. Her sweet reaction stirring all sort of feeling inside me

25th Dec 18.09
So you like it?

25th Dec 18.10
OMG I love it. How did you even know?

25th Dec 18.11
You mentioned it at the bar.

25th Dec 18.11
And you remembered?

25th Dec 18.12
What can I say, you made an impression.

25th Dec 18.14
Hold.

I hold. Like an idiot. Hoping for a picture.

25th Dec 18.17
Are you alone?

25th Dec 18.18
No. But I will be in a sec.

I jump from the couch like an eager teenage boy. The action garners me suspicious looks from everyone in the room. I throw a quick smile at them as I slink out of the lounge and consider my options. I make my way to the bathroom then stop before turning back and going upstairs to my old bedroom. It's the guest room now. All flowery and feminine. All my stuff is gone and all that's left are a few oily marks on the walls where my posters used to hang.

25th Dec 18.24
All alone.

My phone rings and I swipe the screen. Then there she is, all smiles and sunshine. She looks fucking radiant and it almost hurts.

"Hi."

"Hey." I act all casual while my insides riot.

"So, I got your gift."

"So you said."

"And I wanted to show you how it looks."

She puts the phone down and steps back. The *'Limp Bacon'* T-shirt is a size too big, just like she likes it. It reaches to just below her ass and I can see her long, naked legs which make my body stir. Her long hair covers the picture of the lead singer riding a slice of crispy bacon on the album cover, *'I Like It Crispy'*.

"Suits you."

"I love it."

"It matches your crazy."

"Hey!" she pouts, and my cock twitches in my pants. I love her fucking lips. "How did you even get this? These are impossible to find."

"Not for a bounty hunter such as myself."

"Ppffttt," She giggles. "So, you think it looks good?"

"Sure."

"What about now?" In a swift movement she peels the shirt from her body, and it lands in a crumpled black pile at her feet. She is completely naked and utterly fucking gorgeous.

I swallow and lick my lips wishing I could lick her instead. I notice she does the same. "I don't know, I might need a closer look." My cock is already straining in my jeans, and I undo the button then rip my T-shirt over my head.

Twenty minutes later I'm flushed and sweaty, and my mum will have to wash her guest towels. I lie on the bed, catching my breath, and stare at the ceiling. Merry fucking Christmas to me.

∞

גַם

∞

Abi

We landed just after 10 p.m. and I'll probably just make it home just on midnight. The crews are all out, they invited me to join them. Nadav in particular has been nagging. Ever since we broke up and he went back to the wife I didn't know about, he's been overtly nice. He wants me back, or back in his bed. But I have zero interest in him, his advances, or his cock. Spending the night fighting him off doesn't sound like fun. Not when I'd rather be spending it with Seth.

I sigh and look out the window at the unusually quiet highway. Everyone is already where they need to be. While I sit *here* instead of in the place I should be. With him. My stomach knits and rolls and twists like wet yarn. The cool window against my cheek makes me think of the last time he held me. The time he convinced me that this long-distance thing is doable.

I think of the last few months, and my body lights up. Everything about him makes me burn. His text messages, our video dates, the way his face twists and his abdomen hardens and his back bows just before he comes all over himself. Still, I ache. Touching myself for him doesn't fill the void, the absence of him touching me.

The taxi stops at a red traffic light, my gaze meanders to a large lit up billboard. A gigantic sea monster wrapped around a bottle of rum reaching a tentacle towards a small ship that seems to float inside the bottle. My heart stammers and an idea sparks inside of me just as my phone goes off.

1st Jan 00.00
Happy new year Abi. Wish I was there kissing you now.

1st Jan 00.01
Happy new year motek. Hopefully this one will be better than the last.

1st Jan 00.02
What was wrong with the last one?

1st Jan 00.04
I didn't get to see you enough.

He doesn't reply and he doesn't need to because the idea is already growing inside me, spreading like the black ink of the sea monster, and I know, that this new year is about to be amazing.

∞

מחר
∞

3rd Feb 7.33
I'm an uncle.

3rd Feb11.56
Congrats! What is it?

4th Feb 6.44
A baby.

4th Feb 18.23
Seriously? Is it a boy or a girl?

4th Feb 7.45
I don't know I couldn't tell from the pictures.

4th Feb 11.25
Seth!

4th Feb 11.34
It's a boy. They've called him Xavier.

∞

לטעום
∞

Chapter Twenty-One

Seth

My phone pings and I know it's Abi; I know she must be boarding her flight and I hate that she's still so far away from me. I'm not sure how much more torture I can take.

I roll over and grab my phone. The bright screen hurts my eyes, but I still smile at her message

March 3rd 3.46am
Happy birthday I'll call you when you're up.

I'm already up in all the ways that matter and there's nothing she can do about either of those situations. I drop the phone and my gaze bores into the dark ceiling. We've been at it for almost six months, and the fact remains that, although other women have tried to seduce me during this time, none seem to hold a candle to her.

They come in all shapes and sizes, are sexy and sultry and intelligent, and they throw themselves at me uninvited. It would just be so easy to take them and fuck them senseless. But despite everything, they are not her.

She is unmatched on every level. The banter we share, the secrets we hold for one another, the way she carries herself, her strength even in her weakest moments. She takes me as I am, despite all my confessions and drawbacks, she wants me. She hasn't once tried to change me or made me feel judged.

But mostly—it doesn't matter how many times I walk into the bottle'o—every time I see a bottle of rum, my mouth pulls into a stupid grin and my heart pangs and my dick flicks and my whole body knows that it's reacting to something that's just *ours*, that no one else can touch.

I sigh and rub the sleep from my eyes, unsure if I can stop the slew of thoughts that tumble inside me. And maybe all my thoughts are silly ideals, a delusional dream based on a fading memory and broken text messages.

But the fact remains that I miss her. I miss her laughter and her sweet, strange crazy. The way her hand fits into mine and how she laughs at my jokes, even when it looks like she wants to groan. The taste of her skin and the way her body shivers beneath me, and how her eyes screw so tightly before her voice quivers and she clenches around me.

I slam my head back into my pillow wanting the longing to stop; instead, it makes my heart skitter as I think about what a life with Abi might look like.

I run a thousand different scenarios in my head. What if we fight over stupid shit? Like the way she leaves the toothpaste lid open, or the way I leave my work clothes on the floor, or that I leave dishes in the sink till morning.

But the more I think about it, the more my nerves crackle and spit because none of it matters. And maybe I want to fight with her over stupid shit, because when I'm with her, I feel more alive—like every moment is worth experiencing, because she makes even the mundane exceptional.

I want to be wherever she is because she makes me fucking crazy in the best way. I'm done pretending, cause life is short and women like her don't come along every day.

I feel lighter for about two seconds, before the weight I just lifted from my heart comes smashing right back down and fills me with dread. *What if she doesn't feel the same?*

I tell myself that if there's anything that makes me this happy in life, I should grab it with both hands and hold on to dear life. I sigh, feeling like I'm swinging on a noose, choking on my indecision.

∞

את

∞

I must have fallen asleep again. My alarm pulls me from a sweet dangerous dream where Abi feels so real in my arms.

Another full day at work, and then the boys organized a barbeque and drinks at Lachie's. I know it will be a fun night, but she won't be there. I walk around the house feeling like I'm dragging an anchor and check my phone every five minutes like a thirteen-year-old girl. I shake my head and drift towards the shower, hoping to wash some of this pathetic self-pity and wistfulness away. When I'm dressed and back downstairs pulling on my work boots, I hear the pounding on the door.

The UPS man smiles at me when I open it, "G'day mate, Seth Taylor?"

"Yeah mate, that's me."

"Great, sign here please." He holds out the pad and I sign before he hands me a white box, not dissimilar to the one I sent Abi her bottle in.

"Thanks," I take the box and close the door, already ripping the tape. It snags and tangles, and I keep pulling and tagging like a kid opening a Christmas gift—unrelenting and crazed. I yank the tape from the box and throw it in a mangled ball on the counter then tear open the box.

I scatter the wrapping and find a bottle inside. On closer inspection, I notice that it's an identical brand which I sent Abi on her birthday. I wonder if it is in fact the same one I sent, and whether it made its way back across the ocean. It has no liquid, but inside is a paper boat. A delicate origami shape that floats in the emptiness inside. I screw my eyes and look closer. There's writing on the paper. Abi sent me a message in a bottle.

I tip the bottle upside down. The boat won't fit in the thin neck. I shake the bottle and pry my fingers into the mouth just to come up short. Frustration crawls up my skin and I can imagine Abi smirking, thinking she's hilarious. I know she knows I won't smash the bottle, so I set it down and start searching through my tools. I find some wire, create a hook then slide it into the bottle, snag the paper boat and force it through the skinny mouth of the bottle.

I unfold the intricate origami design and a buzz churns through me when I spot the small writing on the inside.

Happy birthday motek sheli,
I've been thinking, I know it's your birthday and you should be the
one asking for things, but this year I'm the one making a wish. See,
I've come to realize we only have one life and it's so fleeting,
anything can snatch it away. Time doesn't stop, it doesn't wait, it
keeps ticking away. We've tried this thing—this long-distance thing
—and though I love you, I'm sick of it. I miss you too much. And so,
I wonder if you'll take a leap with me? I have tickets, one for each
of us for next month, and all you have to do is say yes.
Love Abi.

I read her words over again as fireworks go off in my brain. I clutch the letter in my hand and reach for the phone

as an intense ache ripple through me. I recognize it as longing, and I do long for her. For *all* of her. But it's also relief.
She wants the same thing I want. And for her, I'll leap.

A stupid smile spreads on my face as I call Abi. Of course
she doesn't answer, her answering machine tells me she is
currently unavailable and she will get back to me as soon as
she can; and I believe that stupid mechanical voice as I leave
her my one worded reply.

"Yes."

Chapter Twenty-Two

Seth

My phone pings with an email confirmation of my ticket. A flight to Thailand in just under three weeks. I'd have to sit Jake and Lachie down and let them know they are going to be a man down. Permanently.

I laugh as I think of the ridiculousness of it all—the impracticalities, the obstacles—and yet, somehow none of them matter. All that matters is holding Abi in my arms again and making sure she never leaves.

∞

השפתיים

∞

8th March 17.23
How did they take the news?

8th March 21.23
They like you less.

8ᵗʰ March 23.55
That's ok, I wasn't planning on sleeping with either of
them anyway.

9ᵗʰ March 02.34
Well that's good to know. Can't wait to get my hands on
you pirate.

9ᵗʰ March 07.32
You're going to have to catch me first.

Chapter Twenty-Three
March 27th

Abi

I stand around my empty apartment and scan it for a last time, questioning my sanity. I've given up this amazing space and moved all my stuff into Aba's house. He didn't mind, he had the space. I'm being irrational and illogical; I've quit my job, vacated my house, uprooted my life for a *maybe*, a flicker of an impossible dream; and yet, it feels like the right thing to do. Like meeting Seth was serendipity, and that life was meant to be lived irrationally—like walking into a hurricane. We needed the madness, the fear, the danger, or we risked losing far more than we gained. The winds of uncertainty swirl around me and I embrace them. Eventually, I will reach the eye of this storm and I'd know if I'd made the right decision.

Walking out of my apartment and into the dark corridor, my lungs churn and my heart pounds. My belly knits itself into knots as if I'm running a race, and though I see the finish line, I'm not entirely sure I'm going to win—even when every part of me screams that I should.

Aba waits for me downstairs and places my bags in the

boot. The trip to the airport is silent and allows all the excitement to bubble inside of me.

Maya meets us at the departures area and fusses while I check my bags in, making me double check that I have my passport and boarding pass and sanity. She still treats me like a helpless child.

Maya kisses me goodbye, she still doesn't understand. For the last month, she's repeated how irresponsible I'm being and has asked if Seth has a magic cock. She doesn't believe in the kind of feelings we have for one another. In this invisible thread that's somehow wrapped itself around us and bound us together.

Maya is logical; she follows a straight path, never veering off to the grassy knoll to see what she might find. But I'm a romantic; I believe in the coulds, and maybes of the universe, and will edge to the cliff at the end of the grassy knoll, and I'll peer down. And then I'll jump… even if I shatter a thousand times, I'll still jump—because I'd rather live life plummeting and taking chances than missing that one time I would have soared.

"Are you sure you want to do this?" She draws me into her arms and hugs me tightly.

"Maya!" I scold, and her hot breath tickles my neck as she sighs.

"I'm just trying to look out for you."

"We've been through this. I have to try, he could be the one."

"And if he's not?"

I shrug, "Then I fall."

Her brow creases, "Falling sounds painful."

"It does." My heart shudders at the thought.

"Well then, I hope he catches you before you reach the bottom." She tightens her hold around me for another second before she releases me.

I turn to my dad and slide into his waiting embrace.

"Your mum would be so proud of you," he whispers as his arms close around me.

"She would?" I ask softly and he releases me so he can look at me when he speaks.

"Of course she would. She would have told you to risk it all, because in this life, if there is even a slight chance to grab onto something that makes you happy, you must do it with both hands. Life is too short to die wondering, and happiness is too rare to let go of."

I fall back into his arms, a sob clawing its way up my throat.

"You are so much like her, Abigaili sheli. Now go and don't look back."

He releases me and I wipe away the tears that pool at my eyes, "I love you, Aba."

He nods and stands like a calm, stoic statue, while my insides are a volcano of emotions that I need to keep contained for a few hours longer.

Seth has no idea I'm on the way to him and that we're on the same flight, and he has no idea what else I have in store for him.

Shit. I really do hope he loves my crazy. I'm not ready to break.

∞

שלך

∞

Seth

I look at the clock for the hundredth time. I need to get out of here. My flight leaves in five hours and I still have to get to the airport and check in.

I should have never agreed to take this meeting, but Jake got sick and Lachie is on the other side of town finishing another project. I've already stuffed my brothers over enough so this was the least I could do to help. But as time ticks away, and I still have half a house to measure for quoting, dread begins to trickle through me like an insipid and cold underground lake.

I finish two more rooms to see that another hour has ticked by. Sweat explodes across my brow as I measure out the last room and double check my figures. I can type everything up on my phone later and email it to Lachie, but right now, I need to get out of here.

The owners are nice. They offer me a cuppa which I refuse politely and get into my ute. I'll leave it at the airport's long-term parking. Jake said he'll pick it up in a day or two as long as I foot the bill. I have no choice; I can't afford to go back home to leave it and wait for an Uber, I'll never make it.

I put my foot down and drive like a clown, knowing I'm being reckless. Then again, that's what everyone has labelled me as being in the last month. My parents, my brothers, every mate I've managed to hold onto after the breakup with Jess.

My stomach twists at the thought of her. It's been so long since she's crossed my mind, it's like an ice block sliding down my back. I shudder. The truth is that when I met Abi, whether I admit it or not, I was still all sorts of broken up—shredded and fucked up by Jess and her choices. She fucking destroyed me, tangled me up inside myself and made me feel completely inadequate. A failure. She left me for someone else, and Abi… I thought she was a little bit of glue, a balm to hold me together while I rebounded and erased Jess from my being. Her betrayal stung. It hurt so deep it rattled my fucking bones, and when I got to that airport almost a year ago now, I swore I would never allow myself to get swept away. I wouldn't allow anyone to climb over the walls I've put up and covered with razor sharp wire. And yet, without even trying and without any intent, came this stealthy/crazy woman that scaled my walls uninvited and let herself in; and I didn't even notice she'd done it till it was too late.

I grip the steering wheel as some idiot slows down in front of me and swerve to the right just to see a serpent of red lights wind up ahead of me.

"Fuck!" I shout into the cabin of my ute as I glance at the clock. I'm not going to make it.

I drive at a snail's pace and try like a fool to cut into lanes just to watch the one I left surge forwards. Frustration snags at my skin, and I grind my jaw as I keep watching minutes slip away. When I finally make it to the airport, my shirt is soaked in sweat and my arms hurt from gripping the wheel so hard. I'm sure I'll receive at least two speeding infringements in my mailbox, but I don't give a shit. I slam the door shut, swing my duffle bag over my shoulder and sprint towards the terminal.

My heart chugs in my throat as I scan the departure screen. *I'm not going to make it.* I run into the self-check in counter and type in my information with shaking hands, swearing at the machine for being too slow. My whole body feels like a tight ball of tension as it splutters out my ticket like a drunk hobo. I snatch it and make my way to security. The line is too long, and my stomach drops as I see the words on the screen—boarding closing.

I start begging people in front of me to let me through, they shrug and allow me to make my way up the line. I reach for a blue plastic tray and throw my things on the conveyor belt. Everything inside me feels like it's vibrating, a heartbeat away from imploding, a growing straining frustration. My bag goes through the security check as do I—after removing my shoes and belt—I get redressed, grab my bag, and as I attempt to make my way to my gate, a tall wide man blocks my path. I'm asked to step aside for a random explosive test swab. My knuckles bleed white as I clutch my duffle bag and follow the man. He's slow and meticulous in his movements and I'm ready to burst out of my skin.

He swabs my bag and my jacket before unclipping the sample and entering it into the machine. A small eternity passes as I wait for the analysis. When the machine finally beeps, I feel as though my skin has shrunk and is suffocating me. The man reads the results and wishes me a good day as he stands up in search of his next 'random selection.'

I bolt.

My blood rushes inside my body, surging into my legs, propelling me ever forward. I surge through the terminal, through the leisurely stream of people, slicing a deranged path toward the gate. But even as my lungs burn and my legs scream with pain, I already know.

∞

רק

∞

Abi

A pill has never tasted so bitter or felt so hard to swallow. Dread drips inside me as the cabin crew seal the doors and the terminal empties leaving it deserted. My gaze remains glued to the plane, which pulls away from the sleeve, and the aircraft tug guides towards the runway.

Seth didn't come.

A slow languid wave of disappointment rolls through me, and I bite my lower lip to hold in the whimper that's about to tumble out.

I push away the head dress, suddenly feeling completely ridiculous, utterly stupid, and wildly delusional.

I should have known. I just wanted to believe.

I feel all the magic evaporate from my world—every fairy wing crumple, their magic dust turns to ash, unicorn horns dissolve, and ogres' mud harden as they sink beneath and gasp for air. An unbearable 'I told you so' in Maya's voice echoes inside me, and my chest buckles. I stumble backwards, my hands searching for anything solid. Something to catch me as I fall.

I'm rushing towards the ground. I'm tumbling towards it at light speed. It opens up, threatening to swallow me whole, when a crash from behind me followed by a scream in a low, familiar voice instantly sews the torn seam in my magical reality, and instead of falling, I soar.

∞

שלך

∞

Seth

"No! Wait!" I yell as I sprint and crash into a chair smacking my shin against the metal frame. "Fuck!" I stumble, then rush to the window and watch my flight disappear behind the terminal building.

I look at the empty space where the giant Boeing 747 would have stood not five minutes ago and try to will it back into the vacant bay. Try to wind back time with sheer will power. I slam my fist on the glass, then a second time as I watch a future I have no right wanting, fly away.

Abi would be on another flight now, somewhere over some ocean, and then she'd stand and wait for me at the airport in Phuket. And when I don't show up... I rip my hands through my hair and growl.

"Fuck!" I cry out again and my fist hits the glass for a third time before I let it fall to my side.

I stumble backwards into the row of chairs and fall into a vacant seat. I let my bag drop to the floor and my head collapses into my hands which rest on my knees. My pulse strums in my throat and I slump further into the seat, pulling my phone out. I stare at the screen and wonder what words would appease this stupid move. How I could possibly explain?

∞

לנצח

∞

Abi

I watch him collapse into the seat and sparks fly round my body as if my heart is an anvil being struck by a hammer. It's pure and hot and joyous as I see him despair.

He showed up.

Whatever happened to hold him back no longer matters as I see the anguish and remorse written all over his face. I indulge in his suffering some more, watching him stare at his phone—no doubt wondering how he might explain this mishap to me. He doesn't know I'm here; he was never expecting me. It was part of the surprise. I caught a flight a day early so that we could fly to Thailand together, just like the first time.

I readjust my head dress and grab my phone, slide it open to the camera and check my face. A little red, but the tears that were welling have dried up. Not that it matters, it's all hidden. I make my way to Seth as stealthily as I can.

I watch him, his agony etched in long furrowed lines on his face as he sighs and pinches his eyes shut. He's so focused on his phone a herd of elephants could have run through the terminal and he would be unlikely to notice. The thought makes everything inside me light up.

I approach him tentatively and look down at him. He doesn't look up from his phone.

"Excuse me, is this seat taken?"

His head snaps up so quickly, it's almost comical. His mouth drops open as he takes me in and I swallow hard, my throat suddenly tight and dry.

When he remains silent, I fall into the seat next to him and look around my shoulder, "You look like you could be my next husband."

He stares at me, his eyes growing ever bigger before they

curve at the edges and his mouth falls into a stunning smile, "I'm sorry, I'm not looking for a wife."

I push the white lacy veil from my face and pout in disappointment. "Oh. Well then, what are you looking for?"

He smirks and his sharp jaw twitches as he watches my lips. "A pirate."

I grab his upper arm, feeling the muscles ripple beneath my fingers. My skin tingles as I grab onto his hot flesh, like my body remembers him and everything inside turns on—like a switch has been flicked in a stadium. Light and heat floods my senses. I look around my shoulder a few times, "Is she lurking about? Is she dangerous?"

"She is the deadliest woman I've ever encountered." He keeps playing it cool, though his eyes are rounded and more focused, and he leans in just a little more.

I bite back my smile, "And how do you plan on catching her?"

"I am the world's greatest bounty hunter."

I scoff and cover it up by clearing my throat, "The world's greatest? So how is it she's still free to run around?"

"She is very cunning, but I've set a trap for her. I've got something hard that she can't resist." His voice tightens a little as his hand traces the line of my jaw and his gaze falls to my mouth.

"Oh?" My breathing falters at the touch, anticipation crawls inside me. He leans in a little more, his hand slides into my hair before he releases me completely and turns to his bag. I'm left breathless and wanting while he unzips his bag and produces a bottle with dark liquid sloshing around and a little square box.

It's light blue and topped with a dainty bow. My heart hammers in my chest as he brings the box between us.

He stares into my eyes and mine flit from the box, to his eyes, to his mouth, back to the small box. My stomach somersaults like an Olympic diver and it feels like all my saliva has evaporated.

Seth's fingers slither along the top of the box and he grabs the lid, his eyes shining. He pops the lid up, arresting my breath and my heart for a singular second.

"Would you like some rum?" He says as he holds the box between us. Inside is nestled a shiny shot glass engraved with the same creature that decorates the bottle of rum he's placed on the floor by our feet.

I let out a long breath.

Relief, irritation, disappointment all mixed into one. A turmoil of mixed emotion at his stupid stunt. His lips quiver holding back laughter, and I wonder how many cameras are on us now and if I'd be able to get away with his murder.

My heart chugs at a million miles an hour. I could use a drink to settle me down.

"Yes," I finally say.

"Gotcha," he replies before his lips crash into mine in a feverish, hungry kiss.

Epilogue
Two Years Later

Abi

Seth has his arm wrapped around my shoulder and pulls me closer. He smells like the ocean and suntan lotion and Seth, my three favorite smells. The sun sets behind us as the hustle and bustle of evening swirls in a cacophony of sound.

We wait.

My heart drums in my chest as anticipation leaks into each one of my pores. We've worked so hard to get to this moment, I can't help but smile as I think of our journey. I look up at Seth, he's beaming. Pride rolls off him like a sheen of sweat after we spend the night together.

Our two years together have been amazing, like a dream that some days I'm afraid I'll wake up from. Has it all been perfect? Hell no. We raise hell, we fight, we find out about all the little annoying things we each do and are willing to put up with; but we're perfect for one another, and that's all we need.

Maya stands on the other side of me, her smile brightens up her usual serious face. I got the speech earlier today, the 'I'm proud of you, but you need to remember to be responsible and keep track of things'—forever worrying, perpetually looking after me. I guess this is the way she shows me she loves me.

Jake and Lachie stand on either side of Seth. The three of them look like they belong on the cover of a surf magazine. All ruffled hair and bronzed muscles. I tighten my hold on Seth and grin, I still got away with the best one.

He looks down at my face, "What's funny?" he asks.

"Just happy."

That gets me one of his stunning smiles, and I squirm beneath the heat of his gaze. He dips his head, and his lips graze a whisper of a touch. "Good," he says in his low husky voice, "I like you happy." His lips latch onto mine. My hand slides into his hair, while his slithers down to my ass. I love kissing Seth, I love his hands around me and his body flush against mine.

"Oi, get a room," Lachie's voice cuts through our kiss. "This isn't the show I flew over to watch." Seth's lips leave mine on a smile.

"Yeah, we know what kind of shows you like watching," Jake pipes up.

"Oh fuck off." Lachie elbows him. Jake bursts out laughing while Seth pulls away, his mouth stretched into a smile and his forehead stuck to mine.

"To be continued." He winks then stands to his full height and puts his hand across my shoulder again.

A warm jolt spreads through my body, and I clutch onto him tighter, enjoying his possessive touch and delicious promises.

I turn back to the scene ahead of us. Maya hands me a pair of golden scissors, and I scan the crowd that's gathered around us—our family and friends, as well as curious bystanders. I know eema is watching from somewhere too. My heart gallops with the thought.

The sky darkens and a man with a heavy Thai accent begins the countdown.

Ten,

nine,

eight,

I feel Seth's fingers dig into my shoulder.

Seven,

six,

five,

The scissors shake in my hand.

four,

three,

two,

one.

Seth and I cut the red ribbon just as a huge green neon sign bursts to life, and the crows around us erupts in cheers.

'*Rum on the Run*' flashes at us from above and tears spring to my eyes. The bar we've spent a year building and planning is finally open.

A stream of customers rushes in to explore our new bar. Maya comes in to hug me and Seth's brothers each kiss me on the cheek and shake his hand then walk inside.

We remain outside, stealing a few moments alone to let the sensation sink in. I sigh and lean into him.

"We did it, pirate," he says, then hands me our signature Mai Tai.

"That's because I finally let you catch me, bounty hunter."

He smirks, cups my face and kisses me—a deep, long kiss that says forever.

The End

If you enjoyed this book, please consider leaving a review on Amazon and Goodreads.

The Perfect Mai Tai

Equipment
A shaker
A strainer
Short glass

Ingredients
1 1/2 parts Bacardi Carta Blanco
1/2 part Cointreau liqueur
1/4 part lime juice
1 1/2 parts pineapple juice
1 1/2 parts orange juice
1 dash grenadine
1 part Bacardi Carta Negra
Cubed ice
To garnish: Lime wedge & mint

How to Mix

Put lots of ice and all of the ingredients into a shaker and shake for about 20 seconds to chill the liquid really well.
Strain the mix over ice (you could fill your glass with ice and pour the mix straight in, or – to look extra flash – strain it over ice separately and then add to a glass containing fresh ice).
If you still have the limes you squeezed earlier, use a wedge as a garnish with some mint.

TRANSLATION

Were you wondering what the scene breaks throughout this book were? They were the words to the following poem I wrote, written in Hebrew.

Today I wanted to kiss you,
in the same way I wanted to kiss you yesterday,
and I'm sure to want to kiss you tomorrow as well.
To taste your lips,
just yours,
forever.

ACKNOWLEDGMENTS

A Word From Jane...

I would like to start by thanking you, the reader, so much for reading! If you enjoyed the story, please leave a review and recommend the book to any friend you think would love Seth and Adi's story. You will have my eternal love and gratitude.

To my amazing editor and friend Sarah, you're inspirational and you have all the right words to say when I'm feeling like mine aren't sufficient.

To Kirsty, you know how much you mean to me, thank you for everything little thing you do.

A massive thank you to Tracey Caldwell, your input and encouragement has been amazing.

To K, despite your terrible taste in beverages, you're the best C/P anyone can ask for, thanks for helping me make this book what it is.